ENEMY MINE

Katie Reus

Copyright © 2016 by Katie Reus.

All rights reserved. Except as permitted under the U.S. Copyright Act of 1976, no part of this publication may be reproduced, distributed, or transmitted in any form or by any means, or stored in a database or retrieval system, without the prior written permission of the author. Thank you for buying an authorized version of this book and complying with copyright laws. You're supporting writers and encouraging creativity.

Cover art: Jaycee of Sweet 'N Spicy Designs
Author website: http://www.katiereus.com

Publisher's Note: This is a work of fiction. Names, characters, places, and incidents are either the products of the author's imagination or used fictitiously, and any resemblance to actual persons, living or dead, or business establishments, organizations or locales is completely coincidental.

Enemy Mine/Katie Reus. -- 1st ed.
KR Press, LLC

ISBN-10: 1942447434
ISBN-13: 9781942447436

eISBN: 9781942447429

For my wonderful readers.

Praise for the novels of Katie Reus

"...a wild hot ride for readers. The story grabs you and doesn't let go."
—*New York Times* bestselling author, Cynthia Eden

"Has all the right ingredients: a hot couple, evil villains, and a killer action-filled plot.... [The] Moon Shifter series is what I call Grade-A entertainment!" —Joyfully Reviewed

"I could not put this book down.... Let me be clear that I am not saying that this was a good book *for* a paranormal genre; it was an excellent romance read, *period.*" —All About Romance

"Reus strikes just the right balance of steamy sexual tension and nail-biting action....This romantic thriller reliably hits every note that fans of the genre will expect." —*Publishers Weekly*

"Prepare yourself for the start of a great new series! . . . I'm excited about reading more about this great group of characters."
—Fresh Fiction

"Wow! This powerful, passionate hero sizzles with sheer deliciousness. I loved every sexy twist of this fun & exhilarating tale. Katie Reus delivers!" —Carolyn Crane, RITA award winning author

Continued...

"A sexy, well-crafted paranormal romance that succeeds with smart characters and creative world building."—Kirkus Reviews

"*Mating Instinct*'s romance is taut and passionate . . . Katie Reus's newest installment in her Moon Shifter series will leave readers breathless!" —Stephanie Tyler, *New York Times* bestselling author

"Both romantic and suspenseful, a fast-paced sexy book full of high stakes action." —Heroes and Heartbreakers

"Katie Reus pulls the reader into a story line of second chances, betrayal, and the truth about forgotten lives and hidden pasts."
—The Reading Café

"Nonstop action, a solid plot, good pacing, and riveting suspense."
—RT Book Reviews

"Sexy suspense at its finest." —Laura Wright, *New York Times* bestselling author of *Branded*

CHAPTER ONE

Melina Rodriguez locked the door to the administrative office behind the welcome desk at her veterinary clinic. She'd already secured the kennel area in the back since one of the techs would be staying overnight. Surprisingly they only had a few dogs and two cats being boarded tonight.

As she grabbed her purse off the front desk, the bell to the front door jingled. Even though it was the end of the day and she had no more scheduled appointments, she knew who it was. Knew before she'd fully turned around because she could scent *him*.

The tall, annoyingly sexy vampire who just wouldn't leave her alone had a distinctively earthy smell, but not like her kind. Kiernan Doyle smelled like the ocean, fresh and wild, and he made her crave things she had no business wanting. It didn't seem to matter to him that they were natural born enemies; he was damn persistent. She had a plan to cut his advances short tonight.

She might have made a mistake by sleeping with him almost a year ago, but it was something she'd decided to finally rectify now that he wouldn't take no for an answer. "We're closed," she snapped without turning around.

He made a tsking sound. "If that's how you talk to your patients it's a wonder you're still in business."

"You are not a patient." She turned to face him, then wished she hadn't. Willing her heart rate and breathing to stay normal, she gave him what she hoped was a bored look. It was a little hard considering she'd seen every inch of that hard body naked. Seen it, kissed it, licked it . . . Damn him for being so sexy.

"I could be. If I hurt myself would you patch me up, *doctor*?" His voice dropped a few octaves.

The way he said "doctor" made her lower abdomen clench with a need that scared her. She gritted her teeth and tried to ignore what his presence did to her. Much taller than her, around six foot four, with dark hair that had flashes of auburn visible in the sunlight, and incredibly muscular without being bulky, the vamp turned her on like no one ever had. "Why are you here?" Not that she expected anything from him, but she was surprised he didn't have a gift with him today. Every other time that he'd come to see her he'd brought something for the staff. Last week it had been a gift basket full of muffins, chocolates, cookies, and a bunch of other foodstuff. The week before that he'd brought Starbucks gift cards for everyone, even her part-time administrative assistant. So of course he'd completely charmed everyone she worked with. The man was a menace to her sanity.

Kiernan placed a hand over his heart, and those dark eyes that reminded her of melted chocolate chips glinted wickedly. "All these rejections have me thinking you don't care."

She sighed and placed a hand on her hip. She'd had three surgeries today and had lost a dog that had been hit by a car. Too much swelling to the brain. It had broken her heart to lose an animal, and the pain she'd sensed from the owners had been almost unbearable. Not to mention she'd drained a lot of energy using her natural healing powers. All she wanted was to go home, soak in a hot bath, and get some sleep. "I *don't* care and I wish you'd leave me alone." *Why don't even I believe it?* One night of hot sex should have been easy enough to forget, but she couldn't get the images of their intertwined, naked bodies or his intoxicating scent out of her head.

Instead of teasing her further, concern filled his face. She'd been short with him each time he came in to see her, but it seemed like he sensed she was hurting. "You have a bad day?" he asked quietly.

She nodded, part of her wanting to tell him what had happened. She resisted the urge to open up to him. "What do you want?"

For a moment it looked as if he might push her, but he just stepped back, giving her space. "One dinner. That's all I'm asking for."

The first time they'd met he sure hadn't wanted dinner. He'd just wanted her flat on her back, up against the wall of her hotel room, in the shower.... She mentally shook herself. Thinking about that did nothing but distract her. "Fine."

His dark eyebrows rose for a fraction of an instant, then he smiled, all male arrogance. For a moment she thought she'd made a mistake.

Returning his smile, she took a step forward. "You can pick me up tonight. At my parents' house. My brothers, parents, and probably a few other pack members will be there." *Let's see what he thinks of that.*

"What time?"

She blinked at his question. This wasn't how it was supposed to go. He was supposed to back off. No one wanted to tangle with the Rodriguez pack, the only wolf shifters in Miami and the toughest along the entire East Coast. Especially not Kiernan, member of the Doyle vampire coven, her family's mortal freaking enemies. "Wait, *what?*"

His dark eyes held a knowing look. "What time should I be there?"

"I . . ." No, no, no. He wasn't going to take control

from her like this.

"Cat got your tongue?" he practically purred.

That snapped her out of her stupor. "Two hours from now. If you're late, don't bother showing up. Now if you don't mind, I need to lock up." Without waiting for his response, she brushed past him, vividly aware of his scent and his gaze on her as she moved toward the front door. She shrugged out of her white coat and hooked it through her purse. Even though her jeans and sweater were perfectly respectable, for some reason she felt practically naked in front of him and knew he was staring at her butt. Part of her wanted to be offended, but deep down she enjoyed his awareness and desire for her.

"Like what you see?" she asked, keeping her voice low as she grabbed her leather jacket from the rack by the front door.

All she received was a low growl from Kiernan—one that sounded a lot more animalistic than human. Shivers spiraled through her and she didn't even bother trying to hide it. Not giving into her temptation to turn around, she fished her keys out of her coat pocket and walked outside. He was right on her heels as she locked the front door.

"Aren't you going to set the alarm system?" He frowned down at her as they headed across the parking lot toward her car.

She shrugged. "One of my techs is staying the night. They'll set it. Besides, it's pretty common knowledge I'm the owner. No one's going to risk my family coming after them." She didn't explain further because she didn't need to.

While she might not be one of the physically toughest of her pack, her father was the Alpha and her three brothers were all in law enforcement. No one in their right mind was going to mess with her veterinary clinic. Whether right or wrong, there was a hierarchy in every city or town with shifters or vampires living there. Witches, fae, and demons pretty much kept to themselves, but not shifters and vamps. There was also a hell of a lot less crime in vampire or shifter-run cities. Humans didn't screw around with the supernaturals because the punishment was swift and often brutal.

"Wear your hair down tonight." His voice was low, seductive, and twined around her with a subtleness that had her nipples tightening despite his high-handed attitude.

She was very thankful her coat covered up her reaction. "I'll wear my hair any damn way I please." Instead of coming out harsh, her words were breathy even to her own ears.

He reached out and fingered a loose tendril that had escaped the long braid plaited down her back.

Her eyelids grew heavy for a moment as she remembered what it had been like when he'd run his fingers through her hair, gripped her head in that dominating way as he'd claimed her mouth. She fought to breathe as they stood there, practically frozen.

Instead of responding, he just stared at her for a long moment, then turned and headed to his vehicle. A motorcycle of all things. Even though she wanted to watch him climb onto it—to straddle it with those muscular legs she'd had so many fantasies about since their one night together—she forced herself to slide into the front seat of her car and not look back.

Only then did she allow herself to breathe. Her heart raced and her palms slipped against the steering wheel as she drove out of the parking lot.

What the hell had she gotten herself into? In the past, a few men had tried to use her to get in the good graces of her pack or they'd wanted to use her against them. It had become second nature for her to weed out liars. While her gut told her Kiernan simply wanted her for herself, she couldn't help but question her decision to go on a date with a man who owned a big chunk of Miami—and was therefore competition to her pack's real estate dealings. Someone who by all accounts her family couldn't stand, a man who was a freaking vampire.

***

Kiernan wondered what the hell he was doing as he steered down the driveway toward Amelia and Nevada Rodriguez's home. Apparently he had a death wish.

Anything to spend time with Melina Rodriguez. He couldn't keep the woman off his mind. No matter how hard he tried. At his father's request he'd moved to Miami six months ago and been forced to face the unforgettable woman who'd left his bed in the middle of the night almost a year ago. He hadn't known who she was at the time. His family had a file on her pack but the picture of her hadn't been updated since she was fourteen, almost eleven years before.

That night had been so damn unexpected. He'd driven down from his home a few hours north of the city for business. Afterward he'd gone out for drinks with a friend. Then he'd seen her dancing and had been mesmerized. He'd known she was a shifter, but it hadn't mattered. Need had punched through him like a body blow.

Never in his life had he been attracted to one of her kind before sweet, curvy Melina. He'd been unable to stop himself from approaching her, talking to her, dancing with her.... They'd barely spent an hour together at that club before heading back to the hotel. She'd gotten under his skin. She was sinfully curvy with long dark hair and green eyes he'd stared into as she'd moved over him, riding him with such intensity he could still envision every second of that night.

Then she'd disappeared on him.

But he'd tracked her down even before his father's request that he come to Miami. When he'd found out exactly *who* she was, it had been like a sucker punch to the face, only a thousand times worse.

The Rodriguez pack was strong, large in numbers, and not known for their mercy. Fortunately neither was he or his coven. Even after months of not seeing her, he hadn't been prepared for the almost violent impact of talking to her again, inhaling her scent, touching her soft skin.

But he was a vamp, and she was a shifter—the only shifter he'd ever bedded. Before her, he'd never had anything to do with her kind. He'd never *wanted* to.

If someone had told him half a year ago that he'd soon be pining after a sexy, sensual shifter from the Rodriguez pack, he'd have laughed in their face before kicking their teeth in.

After parking his car—he'd hated leaving his bike at home, but hadn't wanted to piss off Melina before their date even started—he strode toward the front door of the palatial two-story home. The Rodriguez pack had done very well for themselves, as was evident by the string of homes they owned in the exclusive Star Island neighborhood of Miami Beach.

The ornate door opened before he even had a chance to ring the bell. Wearing a skintight green dress that accentuated every single one of her sleek curves, Melina stood staring at him with an incredulous expression—as if she was certain he'd lost his mind.

He glanced at his watch then back at her. "I'm not late." He was right on time.

"I know, I just can't believe you had the balls to show up here," she murmured, her cheeks turning a delicious shade of pink as she grabbed a long coat from the rack by the door.

He glanced past her, surprised her father or one of her brothers hadn't threatened to cut off his balls—or his head. "I thought you said your family would be here."

She swallowed hard and her cheeks tinged even darker. "Um, I lied. Most of my pack is a couple doors down for a meeting. My mom knows I'm going out with you—well, not *you*, but she knows I have a date. And my brothers would probably string you up for even *looking* at me."

"They could try," he said softly, slightly amused

she didn't realize the extent of his power.

She rolled her eyes, as if the thought of him taking on her brothers was ludicrous. He snorted. Let her think what she wanted. After a particular age vampires developed certain gifts and at two hundred years old he'd honed his ability to control fire to perfection. He'd never use it to kill anyone in her family—though before meeting her he wouldn't have hesitated—but if someone came at him he'd sure as hell defend himself.

The drive to the restaurant was torture. Kiernan had to fight to keep his eyes on the road. When she crossed her legs—toned, tanned legs she'd once wrapped around his waist and shoulders—her dress rode up dangerously high, revealing bronzed skin he wanted to cover with his hands and mouth. He cleared his throat as he tried to rid his mind of his fucking fantasies. Too bad it didn't work.

"So what brought you to Miami? I thought you lived in New York." Her voice broke into his thoughts with a husky quality that made every one of his senses stand up and take notice.

"Business." Partially true. His family had sent him down here to check on some of the properties they owned, but he'd been planning to make a trip since he'd discovered Melina's true identity.

"That's not vague or anything. What kind of business?" She shifted slightly against the seat, and he forced his gaze to stay on the road in front of him.

"Did you wear that dress to drive me insane?" he growled.

"What?" She looked down at herself, then at him. The way her cheeks flushed again made his cock jump against the zipper of his pants.

Despite her smart-ass mouth—which he found refreshing—there was an innocent quality to her that surprised the hell out of him. "That dress makes me want to do bad things to you."

There was a long pause in which her sweet honeysuckle scent grew, twisting around him. Finally she spoke, her voice low. "What kinds of things?" That sexy voice held a breathless curiosity.

Despite the night they'd shared together, they hadn't done any of the more erotic things he'd eventually planned. If he answered truthfully she was likely to jump out of the car at the next stop. Or hell, while he was still driving. Instead of traveling down that path, he reeled in his thoughts and libido—sort of—and switched directions. "Do you like dancing?"

She seemed thrown by the abrupt change of topic, but that sweet scent slightly dimmed. Which was good and bad. The more he could smell her arousal, the more his brain short-circuited. "I love it."

"Good." Considering she'd been dancing the night they'd met, he had a pretty good idea what kind of place she'd prefer. He'd picked a low-key restaurant right on the water with authentic Cuban food and dancing. He didn't think she'd appreciate anything pretentious. And he hated that shit.

"That's it? Good? You're not going to continue your earlier conversation?"

Was she trying to kill him? "Not right now."

She sighed and the scent that came off her was a mixture of relief and disappointment. "So how old are you, anyway?"

"Two hundred."

"Oh." A quick glance showed her eyebrows raised.

"Is that good or bad?" he asked wryly.

"Neither. I've just never met a vamp that old. Well, I had never actually met a vampire, not really, not until that night...."

Now that was a surprise, though he knew the night she was talking about. The night he'd met her in a bar, gone back to her hotel room, and had sex so many times he'd been completely drained. Which was the only reason he hadn't heard her sneak out in the early morning hours. "How is that possible?"

Her shoulders lifted casually. "There aren't many vamps living in Miami, and I've never had reason to interact with the ones who do. I grew up very...

sheltered."

Something about the way she said that made him look at her. "Why does that sound more like smothered?"

A small smile tugged at her lips. "I'm the baby of the pack and my brothers are way older than me."

He couldn't bite back the bark of laughter. He didn't have any sisters but he had female cousins and understood perfectly. "I don't blame them. So you were smothered growing up, huh?"

She shrugged. "I'm twenty-five and all my brothers are over a hundred. What do you think?"

Kiernan nodded but didn't respond. The last thing he wanted was to talk or think about her brothers. He knew the only reason she'd agreed to go out with him tonight was because she'd thought she'd scare him off. Since it hadn't worked, he had a feeling tonight might be his only chance with her, and he wasn't going to fuck it up.

"They've always tried to monitor everything about my life; where I went to college, who I dated—"

He didn't realize he'd let out a low growl until Melina stopped talking.

She gave him a sharp look. "Did you just seriously growl at me? I thought only shifters did that."

Kiernan shrugged, not willing to apologize. The

thought of her with other males made all his territorial instincts come clawing to the surface. He didn't care that he had no claim on her. Well, not yet. That was about to change very soon.

CHAPTER TWO

Melina glanced in the bathroom mirror as she dried her hands. She loved the restaurant Kiernan had picked but she'd needed a little breather. The man made her lose her train of thought. Well, that wasn't true. Her thoughts were solely focused on seeing him naked again and having lots of sex, but when she was away from him she could actually think about other things. Like what the heck had she been thinking by coming out with him.

Mentally preparing herself, she paused when the same woman who'd been subtly watching her from the bar area of the restaurant entered the room. She knew what the redhead was, but she wasn't afraid. Even though Melina was young and not as strong as she would one day become—if she lived that long—she could defend herself if necessary. But something told her this vampire wasn't going to attack her in a relatively public place. There might not be anyone else inside the bathroom now but there was always the chance of someone walking in.

"He's just using you, you know." The redhead

spoke as the machine drying Melina's hands cut off.

Turning to face her, Melina lifted an eyebrow. "Is that right?"

The woman's perfect, bow-shaped lips curved into a cruel smile. "Your father—yes, I know who you are—just bought him out of some property downtown. And it's not the first time it's happened. The only reason in the world Kiernan Doyle would be out with a shifter is if he was using them."

"Excuse me." Melina skirted past the woman. She wasn't going to bother with this conversation. Not when the redhead wore her cruelty and maliciousness like a second skin.

The woman laughed and the sound was surprisingly real. "I'm just warning you. Every vamp knows that shifters killed his brother. He hates your kind, though I thought he'd be a little smarter than to go after the youngest daughter of Nevada Rodriguez."

Melina swallowed at the ring of truth in the other woman's voice. "Why are you telling me this?" It certainly wasn't out of the goodness of her heart, that much was evident.

The redhead shrugged. "Because Kiernan's a cold-hearted bastard and whatever he'll do to you, you don't deserve."

Not bothering to say thanks or give any type of response, Melina exited the room and made her way back to the table where Kiernan waited, an easy smile on his face. Easy, yet somehow predatory.

And she knew she was his prey. A few minutes ago that hadn't sounded like such a bad thing. She'd already experienced how great things could be between them and he'd had the nerve to pick her up from her house. Now, however... "Why have you been pursuing me so relentlessly for the past few months?"

His dark eyes widened slightly, the lust rolling off him almost tangible. "I think that much should be obvious."

She didn't respond but bit her bottom lip, trying to work up the courage to ask the question she really wanted the answer to. Yes, the sex between them had been amazing, but she already knew Kiernan had no problem getting women into bed. The thought of him with other women made something dark inside her flare to life, so territorial and possessive she almost jerked back from the intensity of it.

He continued before she could speak. "Now I get to ask a question. Why'd you run from me?"

Her answer was automatic even if it was a lie. "I didn't run."

Dark eyes narrowed. "Then what would you call it?"

She shrugged, hoping the action came off as casual and not jerky. "We had a good night and I knew it was a onetime thing. I didn't want any awkwardness." Not exactly the truth. Okay, not even close.

That night with him had scared the hell out of her. She'd never had a one-night stand before and could count the number of lovers she'd had on one hand—and still have fingers left over. She'd known she was in way over her head the moment he'd kissed her. But she'd been away from home, away from her annoyingly overprotective pack, and she'd wanted to have fun. Kiernan had certainly provided that and then some.

The freedom of being on her own without a dozen different pack members breathing down her neck had made her more than a little impulsive that night. Not that any man would have been fine to warm her bed. She certainly hadn't planned to sleep with anyone. But Mr. Tall, Dark, and Sexy had approached and it had been over for her.

"Why don't I believe you?"

"Believe what you want." She took a sip of her wine, eyeing him over the glass rim. When he didn't respond, just stared at her with those smoldering eyes she could drown in, she nervously cleared her throat. "Did . . . did shifters kill your brother?"

Now he straightened and his face became an unreadable mask. His jaw clenched once before he spoke. "Why are you asking?"

Okay, deflecting with a question. Not a good thing. "Are you using me? Is that what tonight is all about?" Why did she have to sound so damn hurt? She tried to keep the note out of her voice but she couldn't help it. It didn't matter that she'd learned to cover her emotions since the time she was a pup, the thought of this man using her made something deep inside her ache. "Did my father purchase some property you wanted?"

His jaw clenched again and she realized the redhead had been telling the truth. Damn it. Something foreign twisted in her chest, like a silver dagger. The man had made her feel physical things no one else had. Maybe he'd wanted to get back at her for leaving him in that hotel room, and the fact that she was Nevada Rodriguez's daughter was icing on the cake.

"I'm such an idiot," she muttered, standing and grabbing her purse.

One of his hands snaked out, grabbing her wrist. Not hard, but with enough pressure that she couldn't move.

"Let me go," she said through gritted teeth, glaring at him.

"Stay." A guttural growl, practically a demand.

A flush speared through her body at his commanding tone, but she ignored the way he made her feel. "Are you going to answer my questions?"

A quick shake of his head.

"Then I'm not staying." She yanked hard this time, but he let go so quickly she almost stumbled back.

Surprising her, he stood and threw a few bills on the table. Definitely enough to cover their drinks and the meal that hadn't yet been served. "I'll take you home."

"Don't bother." She turned on her heel, not wanting to make a scene. She'd thought tonight would end much differently. Even though she'd been avoiding going out with him for months she'd been excited at the prospect of sleeping with him again. A lot more excited than she'd admit to even herself. A girl only had so much restraint. But she wouldn't be used by someone. If he wanted to get back at her family for some real estate bullshit or some shifter vendetta, no thank you.

As she reached the front of the restaurant he called her name. When she turned she found the redhead from the bar in front of him, her perfectly manicured hand on his chest in a blatantly possessive manner.

To give him credit he looked annoyed, but Melina just rolled her eyes and headed out the front door. Ignoring the valet drivers, she strode toward the first cab in a line of three idling under the giant stone overhang. "Will you take me to Star Island?"

At the name of the exclusive area, the cabbie jumped up from his position lounging against the side of the vehicle and opened the back door for her. "Of course."

She slid into the backseat and restrained herself from looking back. Closing her eyes, she leaned her head against the seat. Maybe leaving so abruptly had been a mistake, but he obviously hadn't been willing to answer her questions and she refused to become a pawn in some stupid game between her pack and Kiernan's coven. She'd had her share of would-be lovers trying to use her against her family—hence her pack's crazy overprotective tendencies. For some reason she'd thought Kiernan would be different, though she didn't know why. Her assumption was based on nothing more than the way he'd made her feel on the one intense night they'd shared together. How stupid was that?

Sighing, she opened her eyes and flipped open her purse. Pulling out her phone, she scrolled down to her cousin Juliet's name. Yeah, she was definitely going to need some girl time tonight, and her cousin was the only one who'd understand. She was the same age and Melina could be honest about who she'd gone out with tonight. If she mentioned anything to her brothers—or worse, her father—they'd probably want to hurt Kiernan.

"Oh shit!" The cabbie's shout and the sudden burst of fear rolling off the human made Melina's head snap up.

Panic shot through her when she saw an SUV barreling down on them. The cabbie had pulled through an intersection and this vehicle was hauling ass straight for them.

There was nothing to do. The cabbie gunned the engine but it was too late. Even though time seemed to slow, everything happened in a split second. The car jerked forward as her driver attempted to get out of the way in time, but the SUV T-boned them.

The sudden impact jarred her straight to her bones. Crunching metal and the cabbie's shouts filled the air as the vehicle shifted. She was thrown across the vehicle, slamming against the side of the door. Spots danced in front of her eyes as she reached out, trying to grasp onto anything for support.

They kept skidding along the pavement under the force of the SUV. After what felt like an eternity, though she was sure only seconds had passed, everything completely stilled and a deathly quiet descended on the interior of the cab.

Melina might heal a heck of a lot faster than humans and even witches, but she wasn't invincible. Stretching out her arms and legs, she tested to see if anything was broken. Blinking away the haze covering her right eye she realized blood trickled down her face. Reaching up she gingerly touched the side of her head and came away with more blood on her fingers.

A similar, coppery scent of someone else's blood teased her nose. Trying to shake off the chill snaking through her body she focused on the man in the driver's seat. "Are you okay?"

He didn't answer.

Unstrapping her seatbelt, she slid across the backseat and reached forward, running her fingers along his neck until she found a pulse. It was faint but at least he had one. Shaking her head she tried to focus on what needed to be done.

Looking around the floor she found her fallen cell phone. Scooping it up, she started to dial 911 with shaking fingers. Smoke billowed up from the front of the cab's engine and from the vehicle that had plowed into them. Briefly she wondered if the other occupants were okay but jerked out of her thoughts when there was a moan from the front seat.

Reaching forward she grasped onto the man's hand, fearful that the crimson streaking down his arm was from a fatal wound. "You're going to be okay. I'm calling for help." Her voice came out scratchy and uneven.

As she started to hit send she realized she didn't know where they were. Melina moved back, hating to let the driver's hand go, but she couldn't see from where she was. Sliding back to the other window, she struggled with the door handle. Finally it creaked open. Brushing her hair back from her face, she stepped out and tripped over her heels, but somehow managed to stay upright. A wave of dizziness washed over her as she took a step.

Before she called she needed to find a street sign, to figure out where they were. As she took a few steps forward she spotted two green street signs, indicating what intersection they were at. Feeling incredibly drained, she pushed the send button. A sluggishness overwhelmed her, threatening to pull her under. Maybe she'd hit her head harder than she'd realized.

Before she took another step two giant arms surrounded her from behind, lifting her off her feet. The viselike grip stole her breath as her cell phone tumbled to the black pavement.

"You're coming with us," an unfamiliar male voice snarled in her ear.

Struggling through a sluggish haze, she tried to

kick back at the man holding her. Her heel connected with his shin, but he barely seemed to notice it.

She tried to breathe but the stranger just squeezed harder, dragging her backward. "Let me go," she rasped out as she tried to fight.

Why wasn't anyone else out tonight? Thrashing out, she began kicking backward as hard as she could. From the intense grip she realized whoever was taking her wasn't human. He was too strong. When her kicks didn't do anything, she slammed her head back.

Pain ricocheted through her skull, but she also injured her would-be kidnapper. His nose crunched only to be followed up by curses.

But he didn't let go. Just continued dragging her backward. She couldn't see where they were going.

An ear-splitting explosion ripped through the air, nearly deafening her.

Her captor let go and suddenly she was falling through the air. Her butt slammed against the pavement, but she didn't stay down long. Rolling over, she pushed up on her hands and knees and struggled to her feet.

A white van twenty yards away was engulfed in flames. Two men spilled out from it, burning. Their screams filled the air as they ran around, arms flailing as they tried to put it out. The man who'd been holding her was running away now. She stared in horror, trying to figure out what was going on, when Kiernan appeared out of nowhere.

He scooped her up then grabbed her fallen phone and purse. "Are you okay, Melina? Talk to me!"

Blinking, she looked up at him as he placed her in the front seat of his car. Fear slithered through her. Were there more kidnappers? She tried to look around but the action made her dizzy. "What happened?" Her question came out slurred.

"Shit, you're bleeding a lot." He reached up and it felt as if he pulled something from her head. Raw agony ripped through her, like silver shredding into her skin.

She'd used so much of her healing powers today at the clinic she was weaker than usual. Otherwise this wouldn't have happened to her. She would have recovered quickly after hitting her head.

Before she could think about asking what was going on, Kiernan's fangs lengthened as he bit into his own wrist. He placed it at her mouth. "Drink." A harsh order.

She shook her head. She wasn't going to drink freaking vampire blood.

"Damn it! You're too weak, Melina. It's either this or a hospital." There was no room for argument in his voice.

Another wave rolled over her, making her dizzy.

While she might be a little disoriented, she knew she did not want to go to the hospital. Her family would flip out and try to keep her under even more lockdown. It had taken so long to get her brothers to chill and let her live a normal life, and she wouldn't give that up. Part of her knew that after this attack, giving up some freedoms was probably inevitable, but she wasn't going to help her family's decision along by taking a trip to the ER.

Vampire blood would give her the strength she needed to recover. Unlike fae and demon blood, which messed people up, vamp blood was full of healing power. Uncaring about the consequences, she latched onto his wrist and sucked. Sweetness, not what she'd expected, slid down her throat as raw strength filled her body.

She wasn't sure how much time passed but she finally pulled back, her breathing harsh and uneven. She couldn't believe she'd just taken Kiernan's blood. That was something she'd dwell on later. "What the hell is going on?" This time the words came out strong.

His expression was dark, deadly. "Someone just tried to kidnap you. I don't know if they have backup, so we're getting the hell away from there."

"But, the cabdriver—"

"I followed you from the restaurant and saw what

happened. I already made an anonymous call to the police." As if on cue, the sound of sirens shrieked through the air.

"But—"

"We're going back to my place until we know who was after you, because, sweetheart, those guys were shifters."

Shifters? Denial instantly bubbled up inside her but she shoved it down because he was right. Even in her previous state she'd scented the underlying animal from her attacker. And not just any type of shifter, but wolf. It had vaguely registered when the man had grabbed her, but she hadn't been thinking clearly. All she'd wanted to do was escape.

The would-be kidnapper wasn't from her pack—that much she was sure of. But if wolf shifters were in town trying to hurt her it could mean they were looking to take over her father's territory and use her as leverage. It was hard to imagine anyone being that stupid, especially when her pack owned and controlled a huge portion of the city, but it wasn't completely out of the question. Dread settled inside her at the thought of a war in her city, her home.

CHAPTER THREE

Kiernan glanced in his rearview mirror as he and Melina tore away from the scene. Getting her to safety was the only thing that mattered. He might be able to harness fire but his gift had limits. If a shifter or human or whoever had been blessed by a witch or the fae, he would be useless against them. Luckily those bastards he'd just smoked hadn't been shielded.

It might be wrong, but he'd taken pleasure in lighting them up. They'd been trying to hurt Melina, a woman he already cared for too much. He was only sorry he hadn't been able to make them suffer longer.

"Did you set those guys on fire with your... mind?" Melina finally spoke again, her voice much stronger than before.

He knew why. For whatever reason, she'd been physically drained after the accident even though she was a shifter. She shouldn't have been so weak, but she had been and he'd had no choice but to give her his blood. "Yeah. It's one of my gifts."

"One of? Holy shit." She turned around in her seat to look out the back window. "Why didn't we wait for the police? My brothers are in law enforcement."

He snorted. "Exactly."

"What's that supposed to mean?" she snapped, anger rolling off her in a violent pop of emotion.

"If they showed up and saw us together, what do you think their first assumption would be? They'd shoot me and ask questions later." A bullet wouldn't hurt him—though a silver one would certainly burn like a bitch—but he didn't want to deal with the fallout of her family. Not yet, not until he and Melina had ironed a few things out.

Her very kissable lips pulled into a thin line but she didn't deny it. Which told him he was right or very close to it. She was silent for another long moment then spoke again, her eyes narrowed. "You could have just waited until right before the cops showed up and left me. I would have been safe."

He shook his head, not believing she could even think that. "If you think I'd ever leave you . . ." *No fucking way.* "Who would be dumb enough to come after you like that?" Kiernan wanted to get straight to the heart of what had just happened. Once he had a name, blood would spill. Her pack could do whatever they wanted, but he was taking care of her.

"I have no idea. There aren't any other packs in the area and I truly don't think anyone would be dumb enough to try to take over my father's territory."

"What about your brothers? Any cases they're working on that might relate to this?" Kiernan had done his homework on the three Rodriguez brothers. One was in vice, the other a detective, and the third worked for a private security firm that specialized in protecting high profile supernatural and human clients.

She shrugged, the action so jerky he knew she'd be coming down from her adrenaline high soon. "I don't know. I need to call my mother." Her voice cracked on the last word and it was like a spear through his heart.

Even though he hated to do it because it meant she might be leaving him soon, he slid out his cell and handed it to her since hers had cracked during her struggle. "Here. Do you want me to take you home or do you want to go to my place?"

She looked at him, green eyes wide with so many emotions. Confusion, fear, and anger. "I . . ." Melina looked down at herself, seeing the blood covering her dress and coat, then looked back up at him. "Your place. I can't let my family see me like this. They'll go crazy. I'll call them once I get there."

Though he wanted to reach out and comfort her, he didn't. Instead he slipped the phone she returned to him back in his pocket. There would be time enough to soothe her once she was safe.

Taking a sharp turn, he cringed when Melina let out a yelp and clasped on to the door.

"Sorry, trying to make sure we're not being tailed." It wasn't common knowledge where he lived since relocating to Miami, so he wasn't worried about anyone waiting at his place to ambush them—not that anyone should know he'd been out with her in the first place. "Did you tell anyone you were going out with me?"

A sharp shake of her head. "Not with you specifically."

That rankled him, but it would help narrow down who had known of her whereabouts. If he had to guess, someone had been watching her neighborhood. Even though Star Island was exclusive and most people thought it was gated, it wasn't. Most people wouldn't mess around with the Rodriguez pack though. They had their own form of security. But that wouldn't stop someone from watching the entrance to the neighborhood and it wouldn't stop someone from following Melina. They couldn't have tailed her home from work, because he had. Some primal part of him had needed to make sure she got home safe.

He'd kept his distance and figured she had no clue,

but that didn't mean someone hadn't been watching her, looking for the right opportunity. He didn't think she'd been a target for very long. If someone had been watching her, he'd have known. A dull throb spread through his skull as he thought of all the possibilities of who could be after her.

After driving all over Miami down various side streets, through the warehouse district, to Coconut Grove and back, he finally pulled into a parking garage three blocks from where he lived.

"This is where you live?" Melina asked, the first thing she'd said in the past half hour.

Hell, she'd probably been questioning her decision to come with him but at least she hadn't asked him to take her home. He would, even if it would go against every possessive instinct he had.

"Not exactly. Take off your coat." He palmed the keys to his car.

"Excuse me?"

"It's covered in blood. You can wear mine to cover up your dress." While he didn't mind seeing the skin tight dress, they didn't need to draw any attention to themselves.

As soon as she'd stripped off the coat and put on his, he threw hers in the closest garbage can of the parking garage. Holding her hand, he was pleased when she didn't pull away, but tightened her grip instead.

A thread of steady fear rolled off her, and he didn't blame her. From her own accounts she'd been sheltered most of her life. While the Rodriguez pack had seen their share of violence in the past century—he knew first hand—she was too young to have taken part of any skirmishes between her pack and other supernatural beings. Hell, she was a vet. She helped animals all day. Kiernan was just surprised she was handling everything so well.

In case anyone had tracked them using traffic cameras—doubtful, but he wouldn't put it past anyone at this point—he knew a route completely free of cameras. Not a straight shot to the condo complex he lived in—it took them twice as long to get there—but it was worth the extra precaution.

"You're pretty paranoid, huh?" Melina asked as they headed into the underground parking garage of the building he actually lived in.

"Careful." At the elevators, he pressed his palm to the biometric scanner and the doors opened.

"After what just happened, I'm not complaining," she murmured.

Melina still held his hand as they entered the elevator, even though she could have dropped it long ago. The knowledge warmed something inside of him he'd forgotten existed. He wasn't supposed to develop feelings for a shifter. For a member of the Rodriguez pack, no less. But he couldn't deny what she made him feel.

The door opened on the top floor. His family owned the entire building and thankfully he was the only one living there at the moment. He wasn't ashamed to be seen with Melina, but he didn't feel like explaining to any of his coven why he was helping a shifter. Not until things between the two of them were settled.

Solidified.

Melina's shoes clacked along the marble floor of the entryway the elevator opened up into. Placing his palm against the other biometric scanner—one that also read his lower vampire body temperature, not just his palm and fingerprints—he opened the heavy metal door and entered first.

He paused for a moment, inhaling scents and listening for heartbeats. A lot of supernatural beings could mask their scent and even their heartbeat, but he was almost a hundred percent sure they were alone. Still, he did a quick sweep of the five bedroom place before retrieving Melina from the front door.

He steered her down the long hallway that branched off toward bedrooms and opened up into the living room. The living space directly connected to a giant kitchen with all new, state of the art appliances—kind of pointless to have considering his kind didn't need to eat. They did and could, especially in social settings to put others at ease, but it wasn't a necessity.

From the amused look on Melina's face he could tell she was thinking the same thing. When she shivered, all traces of his own amusement fled.

Stroking his knuckles down her cheek, he reveled in the feel of her soft skin. "Are you okay? What happened back there to make you so weak?" He'd had to pull out a chunk of glass from her head—the thought made his hands curl into fists—but it shouldn't have weakened her to the point that she'd needed his blood.

Something flickered in her eyes but it was gone so fast he wasn't sure what to make of it. Wrapping her arms around herself, she shrugged. "I was in a car accident."

"There's more to it though, isn't there?"

She swallowed hard and shook her head. "No." She'd make a terrible poker player. Those big green eyes of hers flashed with guilt, but he didn't have the heart to grill her.

Not when she was covered in her own blood and looked ready to fall over from sheer exhaustion. "Come on. I'll show you where the shower is."

Gratefulness filled her expression as she followed him. It only reaffirmed he'd made the right decision not to question her further.

Once she was showered and rested, however, he wouldn't show restraint.

* * *

Melina stood under the powerful shower jets of one of the guest bathrooms in Kiernan's condo. From what she gathered, he lived on the entire top floor. It was only seven stories up, but she didn't plan to go out to the balcony anytime soon. She and heights did not mix.

She'd tossed her dress onto the shiny white tile of the bathroom floor. She almost felt bad because the place was so pristine. Like a freaking hotel. No warmth or personal touches anywhere. Just abstract paintings dotted various walls.

The warm water coursing over her was like heaven. Thanks to Kiernan's blood she felt almost like new. A little tired, but not like she should have been. For a moment she'd been tempted to tell him about her natural healing abilities but had held back. It wasn't common knowledge and her father would be incredibly angry if she told a vampire about it.

The upside of her gift was that she could heal

most animals, humans, shifters, and pretty much any supernatural being—unless they were too far gone like the sweet mastiff from earlier that day. In worst case scenarios it drained her to the point of incredible weakness, and it took a long time for her to heal. It was the reason she'd become a vet as opposed to entering another medical field. Healing animals didn't drain her nearly as much as other beings did.

Once she was sure all the blood was washed clean, she stepped from the giant glass and stone enclosed shower and slipped on the fluffy blue robe Kiernan had left for her. Since it was almost her size and definitely too small for him, she wondered who it belonged to but pushed down the unfamiliar feeling of jealousy.

Kiernan had the ability to make her claws unsheathe without doing a damn thing. All she had to do was think about him with another woman and she was ready to claw someone's eyes out. It went so against her personality it shocked her to her core.

"Find everything okay?" Kiernan's deep, familiar voice made her jerk around from drying her hair at the mirror.

She placed a hand over her chest. "I didn't even hear you." That surprised her. With her heightened senses she should have, but she'd been too wrapped up in her own thoughts.

His dark gaze traveled from her face, practically caressed her covered breasts, then dipped all the way to her painted pink toenails.

Unable to stop her physical reaction, her nipples beaded almost painfully. Almost as if he knew, his lips curved up slightly as his eyes landed on her face once again. "I turned this back on and it's been ringing nonstop since you got in the shower." Sighing, he held out her cracked cell, as if it was the last thing he wanted to give her.

Frowning, she took it, looking at the cracked face. "I didn't think it was working."

"I didn't either. Looks like it just got turned off in your struggle."

She'd need to replace it but she was thankful it worked. Now she could at least call her family and tell them she was all right. After what happened she knew she should probably go home to the safety of her pack, but she didn't want to. They'd keep her under lockdown and she loathed the thought of living like that. At least with Kiernan she'd have some freedom. "Do you think . . . I could stay with you?"

His eyes darkened to a midnight black as he nodded. He growled low in his throat in answer.

Something about that look made her entire body flare to life. She'd been on the receiving end of his focus once and it had threatened to overload her senses. To find herself there again made her body tingle in raw sexual awareness. But first . . . "Did you plan to use me because of my family?"

"No." The answer was so immediate she had no doubt of the truthfulness. Not to mention she couldn't smell the bitterness of a lie. His next words surprised her. "What I want from you has *nothing* to do with your pack. And when I think about you, I'm sure as hell not thinking about anyone else. I don't like shifters—or I didn't until I met you. It's not exactly a secret, but I don't want to use you. At least not in the sense you're asking about. However, I do plan to use your body for all sorts of . . . things."

Things. The dark note in that single word sent an erotic thrill through her. One that made the heat between her legs grow until all she could think about was taking off her robe, stepping into his arms, and letting him push deep inside her. Considering the way he was practically undressing her with his eyes she knew he wouldn't reject her. Before she could contemplate anything, her phone buzzed in her hand. The number on the screen surprised her. It wasn't a member of her pack, but Irene, a human woman from a homeless shelter downtown. Melina knew her friend wouldn't call in the evening unless it was an emergency.

She immediately pressed the talk button. "Hello?"

"Melina, thank God! I need your help. One of the teenagers who bounces in and out of the shelter has been shot."

Hating that Kiernan could hear every detail of their conversation thanks to his extrasensory abilities, she turned to the side, trying to give herself the illusion of privacy. "Why haven't you called the police?"

"He's here with two of his friends. They both have guns and are refusing to let me call the cops. They're not going to hurt me but they said if I tried to call the cops they'll leave. He doesn't have much time and I thought . . ." Her voice broke. "He's hanging out with the wrong crowd—local gang members—but he's such a good kid. I thought maybe you could help him with your gift." She whispered the last part.

Irene was one of the few people who knew what Melina could do. She volunteered with the other woman, and Melina had needed to use her healing powers more than once in Irene's presence. Not even Melina's pack knew the human was aware of what she could do, and she planned to keep it that way.

Shooting Kiernan a glance over her shoulder, she bit the inside of her lip. "Give me fifteen minutes."

"Thank you so much. Use the kitchen entrance at the back, that's where we are."

After hanging up, Kiernan gave her a dark look.

"You're not going anywhere. Not with shifters out to kidnap you."

"I have to. I'm sure you heard my conversation." He nodded. "Then you know I have to go. Do you have any clothes I can wear?"

Growling under his breath and sounding more like a shifter than a vampire, he turned, motioning with his hand for her to follow. Hurrying after him she followed him to what she assumed was another guest room. It wasn't covered in his distinctive, wild scent.

He jerked open a door to reveal an oversized walk-in closet. "I don't know what's in here but it belongs to some of my cousins. Just grab what you need." Crossing his arms over his chest, he leaned against the door frame as if he planned to watch her.

"Uh, I need to get changed."

"I guess you better hurry then." His voice was full of sin and sex.

She could waste time arguing with him, but decided to just drop her robe. There wasn't time, something he knew and was capitalizing on. She couldn't really fault him because if she had a chance to see him naked again . . . No time to go there.

Kiernan sucked in a breath behind her as the thick robe hit the floor. She smiled to herself. Served him right for refusing to leave. Feeling incredibly exposed, but also powerful that she could evoke reactions from a vampire as sensual as Kiernan, she grabbed a plain long-sleeved black T-shirt and tugged it over her head. She was very aware that she wasn't wearing any underclothes but she didn't see any lying around. She didn't relish the thought of wearing a stranger's underwear anyway.

After shimmying into a pair of dark jeans, she turned to find Kiernan had gone impossibly still. She felt her cheeks heat up at the blatant lust in his eyes. He looked like he wanted to take her right on the closet floor. "You insisted on staying," she said quietly.

"I did."

She swallowed hard but forced her eyes away from him and onto the closet floor. The space was packed with a ridiculous amount of name brand clothing, purses, and thankfully shoes. She scooped up a pair of flat boots and slid them on. It felt weird without socks but oh well. They needed to be gone ten minutes ago. "Thank you for taking me."

He gave a curt nod as he exited the closet with her. Wearing all dark clothing and with his height, he looked so damn intimidating she was glad he'd be with her facing the gang members. Not that she worried about some human kids being able to hurt her, but some of those kids got jacked up on fae or demon blood. It not only gave them super strength, it made some of them go out of their heads.

"So what's this gift your friend was talking about?"

She shrugged as he opened the front door into that gorgeous marble entryway. "I'm a doctor. I might work on animals, but I've helped her before with some of the kids from the local *barrios*. They're too afraid to call the cops and they know Irene won't narc them out to anyone. If she trusts me, they'll trust me too."

He shook his head. "I can't believe your father is okay with that."

Shooting him a quick glance, she gave him a tight smile. "He doesn't know."

Jaw tight, he just shook his head. The elevator dinged as they reached the ground floor and she resisted rolling her eyes at him. She did not need another male in her life telling her what to do or judging her actions. He stopped in front of a car.

"What's this?" she asked.

"All these vehicles are property of my coven." He swept his hand out at the array of vehicles in the underground garage.

"Nice." She slid into the passenger side of an older model Mustang. At least they'd be riding in style, though if she was honest, she really liked his motorcycle. Her phone buzzed in her pocket, and a look at her phone made her wince. It was her mother and way past the time she was supposed to check in.

She might be an adult, but since she was going on a date with a vampire that night, she'd made sure her mother knew. That conversation had been one big argument. Of course she'd left out Kiernan's name. Her pack and his coven had a certain level of animosity toward one another, due to some feud from almost a century ago. It was way before her time and she really didn't care what it was about. She might not be completely sure about Kiernan's motives, but she knew he wouldn't hurt her. Not physically, at least. Instead of answering, she rejected the call then typed in a quick text telling her mother she was fine but staying out the entire night. She also entered their code word so her mom knew it was her and not someone pretending to use her phone.

The curt response she received told her to call immediately. Melina slid her phone into her pocket instead. After she helped the kid at the shelter, she'd call. Until then she didn't want to deal with any other distractions. Especially not when she had a giant, very sexy one sitting right next to her.

CHAPTER FOUR

Kiernan parked behind Helping Hands, the shelter Melina directed him to. The expansive two story building took up an entire city block. This was the last place he wanted to be. Out in the open, exposed. He hated bringing her here, but he knew when to pick his battles. The moment they stepped out of the vehicle, he knew they weren't alone. Two distinctive heartbeats were very close by. He heard others in the vicinity but these two were very close.

Two teens, one black and one white, stepped out from behind a Dumpster. Each had a gun held loosely in his hand, and from the bulge under one of the teens' T-shirts, Kiernan knew he was packing more. Immediately he stepped in front of Melina, blocking her body with his. As a shifter she should be able to heal almost as fast as him, but something about her had been different after that car accident. She'd been too weak, almost disoriented. He bared his fangs at the two youths before they even had time to raise their weapons.

With wide eyes they stared at them. One cleared

his throat. "You're Melina, right? You're here to help Raul?"

Melina peeked around Kiernan. "Yes. Hand those weapons to my friend here and you can come inside while I help Raul."

For a moment it looked as if they might argue, but after another look in Kiernan's direction, they did as she said. There were certain laws in any jungle, even a concrete one, and Kiernan could kill these two in seconds whether they had weapons or not. And they knew it.

Kiernan cleared his throat when they only handed him the two visible guns. "All of them."

The white boy cursed but handed over his other gun as the door flew open. A tall, attractive blond woman Kiernan assumed was Irene rushed out. She gave the boys a quick glance before zeroing in on Melina and Kiernan. She stopped short as she looked at him. "Melina, who is this?"

"He's fine, trust me." Brushing past him, Melina let her friend guide her inside into an industrial-sized kitchen that smelled of cleaning supplies and the faint aroma of lasagna.

Kiernan stayed close, conscious of the two boys following them, but not worried about the young humans.

"What happened?" Melina asked as she stopped in

front of a young teen maybe eighteen years old stretched out flat on his back on a large metal table likely used to prepare food. Blood spilled profusely from a wound in his shoulder, dripping onto the shiny surface and trailing to the floor below.

Kiernan's fangs faintly ached at the coppery scent. He'd learned to control his bloodlust over a century ago but some things were biological.

"Shadow shot him," the black kid said.

"Shadow?" Irene asked as Melina pulled away the cloth that had been pressed against the wound.

"Yeah. His real name's Clyde. That's just his street name," the same kid spoke again, obviously the spokesperson of the two.

"Why'd he shoot him?" Kiernan asked this time.

The same kid eyed him for a long moment then shrugged. "Raul went after him because Shadow was messing with Raul's little sister. She's fifteen, man." Another shrug.

Kiernan looked back at Melina as he spoke to the kid again. "When you say messing with her . . ."

A snort. "What the hell you think I mean? He tried to rape her."

Now his fangs ached to unleash for a completely different reason. "What's Clyde's last name?"

"Bricker," the kid said after a short pause.

Kiernan filed that information away as he

watched Melina work. It was obvious this wasn't the first time she'd helped her friend considering the display of medical supplies already laid out. She cleaned and disinfected the wound with an impressive quickness.

"You're lucky this went all the way through," she murmured to her patient. To give him credit, he hadn't uttered more than a few cursory groans.

As she finished cleansing him, Irene turned to the other two boys. "You two need to wait outside now."

They left without argument. When Irene turned to him, as if she planned to tell him to leave too, Kiernan shook his head. All his territorial instincts roared to the surface at the thought of leaving Melina, even for only a moment. "I go where she goes."

Melina shot him an exasperated look over her shoulder. "You need to wait outside . . . please." She tacked on the please as if it pained her.

Kiernan just raised an eyebrow and tapped his wrist, as if he had a watch on. "Time's wasting. You can argue with me or . . ." He shrugged, knowing it would drive her crazy, but he wasn't leaving her side.

She opened her mouth once as if to argue then growled at him. For the first time since they'd met he could tell she was truly annoyed with him. "Damn it, Kiernan—"

"I am *not* leaving." There must have been something in his voice that convinced her he was serious because after a few seconds ticked by she sighed and turned back to the young boy who'd finally passed out.

Kiernan blinked as a soft blue glow seemed to completely encompass the teenager. It spread out from his hands where Melina grasped him, moving to his arms, across his torso, spreading everywhere. It seemed to come from inside him, pushing out warmth like a dim nightlight.

Melina's eyes were closed, her expression serene, her body preternaturally still. If he couldn't hear her heartbeat and see the soft rise and fall of her chest he'd be worried about her.

Kiernan was silent as he stared at the two of them, finally understanding why Melina had been so drained earlier. She was a healer, a being so rare they were revered among all supernatural species. It wasn't in his coven's file on her family—though that hadn't been updated in over a decade—so he surmised this was a guarded secret. Healers were treated with respect across all species. It was an unwritten rule. They were never targeted or harmed even if factions were battling each other.

After ten long minutes she drew her hands back, looking pale and drawn and ready to collapse. "He should be fine now. It wasn't a bad wound to begin with."

The wound was now almost completely healed. A red puckered mark about an inch in diameter remained on his shoulder. She carefully placed a couple steri-strips across the raw skin, but he doubted they were even necessary.

Kiernan left the weapons on one of the counters, deciding to let Irene do what she wanted with them. The second Melina finished he sidled up next to her, wrapping his arm around her shoulders. He liked touching her, being able to support her even in a small way. To his surprise she didn't fight him. Instead she turned into him and slid her arm around his waist using him for support.

"Thank you so much, Melina," Irene said. "I'll clean up everything and make sure the boys don't mention your presence here to anyone."

Kiernan bit back an angry retort. This was the last place Melina should be, especially without her pack's protection or knowledge. If there was one thing he respected about shifters, it was that they took care of their own.

But if she did this kind of thing without her pack's approval, he knew he was the last person she'd listen to. He was just glad he'd been able to go with her. She was in no condition to drive right now and if she'd been alone... He shoved that thought away and they left.

Gently, he helped her into the passenger seat, ready to get as far away from the shelter as possible. He wanted her under lockdown.

"How would you have gotten home if I hadn't been here to drive you?" he snapped, the words coming out harsher than he'd intended. He wanted to tell her how amazing she was, how much he respected what she was doing, but it scared him knowing she could have been out on her own in such a weakened state.

Sighing, she turned in her seat to face him, her eyes heavy-lidded. "Irene would have taken me or one of my female cousins would have picked me up." Another tired sigh. "They're the only ones willing to go behind my father's back." A soft, sweet chuckle.

"So you're a healer." Not a question. Keeping one hand on the wheel, he reached out with his other and stroked his knuckles down her cheek.

"And you're very sexy," she murmured.

Surprised, he shot her a quick glance before averting his gaze back to the road. She was definitely tired and out of it to blurt out something like that. Even though it was underhanded he decided to get some answers while she was in this state. Something told him she'd be more open when she was so languid. "So you didn't realize who I was at that club we met in?"

Her sleepy eyes blinked slowly as she shook her head. "Nope. Not until you took your shirt off. Saw your family crest tattooed on your chest. Realized exactly who you were then. Morgan and Oriana Doyle's son. My parent's freaking enemies," she muttered, the words barely audible.

There was nothing but pure truth in her voice. He noticed the way she said her parents, not her pack and not herself. A strange feeling of relief slid through him. "You don't view my family as your enemy?"

She shifted in her seat, laying her head back against the headrest and closing her eyes. "Why would I? You've never done anything to me."

Melina kept surprising him. It was obvious she didn't know the full extent of the violent history between their families. Which made sense. She was only twenty-five. Most of his young cousins weren't aware of the violence that had passed between his coven and their pack because it had all been buried and settled well over a century ago. They didn't even live in the same vicinity. Well, until now. His father had decided to start scooping up real estate in Miami after the recent plunges in the market. While it was smart from a business standpoint, it was also playing with fire considering the Rodriguez pack made their home here.

Still, it bothered him. "You didn't think about walking away when you saw my crest?"

She let out a soft laugh that went straight to his aching cock. "You were practically inside me when I saw it and I definitely wasn't backing out then. No more questions," she said on a tired sigh.

He was done with talking too. As he steered into the parking garage he made a decision he knew was going to change his life. Though he'd already done it once in an emergency, doing it a second time meant something to his kind. To him. Piercing the skin on his wrist with his fangs, he opened a vein and held out his arm for Melina.

"Drink," he ordered.

Her eyes fluttered open. She looked at him, then their surroundings. "I'll be fine by tomorrow morning."

"I don't care. *Drink.*" Some deep, dark part of him needed her to take this from him. It was like an ache inside him, a burning need to take care of her. Seeing what she'd selflessly done tonight, he wanted to at least do this. "Please."

At his last word, her green eyes widened. For a long moment insecurity flared in their depths, but she tentatively grasped his arm with her delicate fingers and held his wrist to her mouth. Her lips were warm against his skin, her tongue a velvet caress that made the blood surge hotter through his veins. The feel of her tugging on him, drinking from him, sent erotic waves coursing through his entire body. He rarely let anyone drink from him, and never a shifter, but now he'd allowed her to twice in the past few hours.

After more than a few long pulls, she tilted her head back, slight embarrassment in her eyes as she looked at him. "I can't believe I did that. *Why did I do that?*" she asked, but it was obvious she wasn't looking for an answer from him.

"I'm glad you did. How do you feel?" He sealed the punctures in his wrist with a quick swipe of his tongue before reaching out to cup her cheek.

No longer were those green eyes tired or dull, but bright and wide. She didn't pull away from him, but leaned into his embrace. His entire body tightened, his muscles pulling taut as he imagined sinking himself inside her again.

"Amazing.... What are we doing?" she asked quietly.

He knew she wasn't referring to what they were doing at that moment. "I don't know, but I haven't been able to get you out of my mind since that night."

"Me neither. You're the first vampire I've ever..." She trailed off, her cheeks tinging pink.

A low growl built in his throat. "First or only?"

"Only."

Her answer soothed a primal part of him so he decided to be honest with her. "You're the only shifter I've been with. And I haven't been with anyone else since you."

Melina pulled back from his light embrace of her cheek and snorted. "You don't need to lie."

"I'm not lying." The words came from a dark part of him.

She must have heard the truth of his words because she nodded once as if to confirm she believed him, but didn't say anything else. Just grasped the handle and stepped from the vehicle. The sweet honeysuckle scent rolling off her left no doubt in his mind what she wanted at that moment.

He wanted it too. No matter how stupid this was or what the consequences of a relationship with her could bring. He wanted her so bad his entire being called out for her. Like a magnetic pull, he'd felt it that night in the bar. Almost like he'd been drugged on her scent. It had just been a physical draw then, but now... he wanted more than just another night with her.

Melina was barely aware of them going up the elevator and into Kiernan's condo, but minutes after arriving she found herself sitting on one of the counters in the kitchen. Unfortunately she was still clothed as she watched him rummage through a nearly empty pantry. Eventually he came out with a box of energy bars.

"I'll stock up tomorrow but this is the only decent thing in here."

She smiled as he unwrapped then handed her the bar. "I'm fine, really." And she was, thanks to his blood. It still stunned her she'd taken his wrist so easily but it had been impossible to turn him down and just as sweet as the first time she'd taken from him. Everything about him lit her body on fire.

"Eat, please." He nestled his way between her legs, forcing her to spread them wider.

She could feel her cheeks flame at the way his voice dropped seductively low. "I can't eat with you staring at me."

"Fine." Leaning down, he nuzzled her skin, lightly raking his teeth over the column of her neck.

Grinning she took one bite of the bar before tossing it onto the counter. Eating was the last thing on her mind now. She knew this was probably a stupid move, especially when she had a whole mess of things to worry about—like who had wanted to kidnap her earlier—but in Kiernan's arms it was hard to think about being responsible. Hell, it was hard to think about anything at all.

She wrapped her legs around him and grasped his thick hair with one hand. He was strong enough that if he didn't want to move, he wouldn't have. But he let her pull his head back so she could kiss him.

His lips covered hers, his tongue invaded her mouth, and she felt each stroke and lick straight to her core. The heat between her legs grew with each stroke as she imagined him teasing her there in the same way he was teasing her mouth.

When his hands slid under her T-shirt she didn't regret her decision to stay the night with him. Large, strong hands slowly crept their way up her stomach then ribs until possessively covering both her breasts.

He tore his mouth away from hers only to tug her T-shirt over her head. Instead of resuming his kisses, he stared at her with such a hungry look it sent tingles to all her nerve endings. "I've fantasized about your breasts for an entire fucking year." The statement was almost accusing.

She followed his gaze to her light brown nipples, which were rock hard in anticipation. He didn't disappoint. When his head dipped toward her breast, she arched her back, ready for the pleasure he could give her.

The moment his tongue flicked over her nipple, her inner walls clenched with an unfulfilled need.

Her entire world rocked on its axis as an explosion ripped through the air. Glass shattered and metal bent in a torrent of noise. Panic punched through her, a vicious blow hitting all her nerve endings.

Kiernan yanked her off the counter and shoved her down behind the cabinets as a flash of lights and another bang popped around them.

The sound pierced her eardrums and she blinked trying to understand what was going on. Terror forked through her. They were under attack.

Then she scented them.

Her brothers.

Oh shit.

"Kiernan!" she shouted, trying to be heard above the next bang, but he kept her pinned down under him, protecting her with his body.

That's when she saw the growing flames around them, spreading outward in a giant circle, covering the tiled floor and part of the counter. It was the same fire that had burned those two men and that van.

"Melina!" She heard Carlos's voice over the din of

noise. He was the youngest of her three brothers, though at one hundred and fifty he was a lot older than her and very powerful.

"I'm fine! Don't hurt Kiernan!" she managed to get out under the weight of Kiernan's hulking body. Damn he was strong.

Kiernan moved off her so quickly she could barely catch her breath. She watched as he jumped up and over the counter that led into the attached, open living room.

The fire that had been licking the tile went with him. She watched the bright orange flames dance over everything, but not actually burn anything. Though the heat was powerful and very warm, there was a perfect circle surrounding her by a few feet. Protecting her.

The sounds of shouts and growls tore through the air. Panic jumped inside her, a raw, living thing. Following Kiernan's lead, she jumped to her feet but jerked to a halt at the sight in front of her. Kiernan stood on the coffee table in his living room, flames bright and angry all around him, keeping her brothers at bay. Her three brothers surrounded him, all toting weapons including a freaking crossbow.

"Stop it! All of you, stop this instant!" she screamed.

Instantly the fire dimmed though it didn't completely extinguish. Her brothers turned to face her. She could feel the heat creeping up her neck as she kept her arms crossed over her chest. They all stared at her, wide-eyed, except Kiernan. His gaze was on Miguel, almost daring her brother to make a move.

"Do not move," she snapped before ducking back down behind the cabinets to grab her discarded T-shirt. Once she'd tugged it on, she popped back up and hurried around the counter that separated them.

As she walked farther into the living room she realized her brothers had thrown flash grenades into the room after busting out the windows. How they'd even gotten inside considering how high up the floor was she didn't even want to know. Though the black rope and hooks dangling around their waists gave her a pretty good clue.

"What the hell are you all doing?" She stared in horror at the three of them. "Do you want to start a war with the vampires?"

"I got called to an accident scene and I scented your blood, but you weren't there. Then Mom told us you were out with a *vampire.*" Miguel shot an accusing look at Kiernan. "What the hell is going on?"

Before Melina could answer, Kiernan moved to stand next to her using his supernatural speed. When her brothers growled and all took menacing steps forward, his flames grew into a thick wall separating her and Kiernan from them.

She grasped his forearm. "You're not helping," she said quietly. While she knew he was just trying to protect her, she also knew her brothers thought they were here to help her.

He remained silent, his gaze on Miguel. The intensity of Kiernan's look shocked her to her core, but she ignored it for the moment and turned back to face her brothers as the fire dipped to tiny flames.

"I was in an accident—well, it wasn't an accident. I'd planned to tell you later tonight." After she'd had sex with Kiernan. *Yeah, better leave that part out.* "Someone plowed into the taxi I was in and they tried to kidnap me. Shifters, but I didn't recognize them. How's the cab driver?"

Miguel shook his head, his expression grim as he stared Kiernan down. "It's touch and go."

A heavy weight settled on Melina's chest. Normally after healing people she was so drained she couldn't get out of bed for days, but thanks to Kiernan she felt better than ever and wanted to visit the hospital. Maybe she could help the driver.

"So what are you doing *here?*" Now Roberto spoke, his voice dripping with disdain.

Melina didn't plan to go into detail about how she'd left the restaurant without Kiernan. "Kiernan saved my life when *shifters* tried to kidnap me."

All of her brothers looked shocked at that but before they could speak, Kiernan cut in. "How did you even find this place?" His voice was a razor sharp edge.

Roberto flicked a glance at Kiernan before looking back at her. "Dad put a GPS tracker in your phone."

"*Again?*" She'd disabled the built-in GPS system that was so common in cell phones, but her father kept putting actual trackers in her cell. And she kept removing them. She'd also checked this morning and there had been nothing there.

Her eyes narrowed but her brother held up a hand. "This one's different than the others—small, practically untraceable. We would have tracked you down sooner but you've been moving around. And this place wasn't easy to get into."

After leaving the homeless shelter Kiernan had pretty much taken a tour around the city in case they were being followed. She hadn't thought she had to worry about being tracked by her phone or she would have tossed it. While she was grateful her family loved and cared about her, she hated feeling like she never had any freedom or privacy.

Even though she wanted to stay with Kiernan and finish what they'd started more than she wanted her next breath, she knew it would only exacerbate the situation. Placing a gentle hand on Kiernan's forearm, she lightly squeezed. "I need to go with my brothers."

His jaw clenched impossibly tight as he stared down at her. So many emotions swirled in those dark eyes, but she couldn't get a handle on any of them.

Before he could speak, Miguel growled, "Get the fuck away from my sister."

Kiernan's head snapped up. "Or what?"

"Or I'll do to you what I did to your brother."

Kiernan hissed in a sharp breath of air and his muscles flexed underneath her fingers. He didn't move toward her brothers but she could feel the energy pulsing off him in scary waves as the flames flickering along the tiled floor jumped about a foot.

Ignoring her brothers, she focused on Kiernan. There was a raw energy, an almost pained expression on his face she wanted nothing more than to wipe away. "What's he talking about?" she whispered even though everyone in the room could hear her.

"Miguel killed my older brother about a hundred years ago." His voice was so monotone, so devoid of emotion she knew he was holding all of it in.

All the air sucked out of the room with that one statement. Her fingers clenched on his arm, his words punching into her chest with an almost tangible force. "What?"

Instead of answering her, he turned back toward her brothers. "I'll let you take your sister, but if you ever come into my place uninvited again, you won't be walking out."

Melina clutched his arm, desperate for answers, to understand what had happened between their two families. But he stepped away from her, severing their connection.

The action pierced her like a silver dagger through the heart. Though she wanted to stay, to force him to talk to her, she knew it wasn't the time or the place. She had to diffuse the situation with her brothers before it reignited.

Shaking off the arm, Carlos—the only one of her brothers who had been completely silent except to shout her name when they'd stormed the condo—tried to wrap around her shoulders, she stalked down the hallway that led to the front door. "You're paying for all these damages," she said under her breath as she yanked the door open. At least going downstairs didn't require a biometric scanner.

She couldn't believe the assault her brothers had just launched on Kiernan's place, but what really stunned her was his admission about Miguel killing his brother. The almost stricken look on his face haunted her.

A hollow, bereft feeling settled in her chest as she stepped inside the elevator. As soon as she talked to her brothers and worse, her father, she and Kiernan were hashing things out. She might have run from what he made her feel once, but that was then.

Now things were different.

He'd pursued her for months and he didn't get to make her want and feel and start considering the possibility of letting him into her life then turn away from her because of her family and their stupid vendetta. She refused to let that happen.

CHAPTER FIVE

Melina sat in her father's study reeking of smoke—thanks to those stupid flash bang grenades—and, of course, *vampire* as she waited for her Alpha to interrogate her.

She'd ignored her brothers on the way home, even Carlos, which she felt a little bad about. They'd always been closest, but right now she was livid at her overbearing pack. Worse, she knew they were going to use the attempted kidnapping to keep her under lockdown. She was all for safety and precautions, but she didn't want her veterinary practice to suffer and she didn't want to live like a prisoner. If she hadn't used so much energy using her healing powers before she would have been better prepared to defend herself. She might not be the strongest in the pack, but her brothers had taught her to defend herself.

The heavy oak door opened then closed behind her. Melina didn't turn from her seat in the high-back chair in front of her father's desk, but waited for him to take a seat across from her.

Surprising her, her father, all six feet three inches

of him, sat in the matching brown high-back chair next to hers and shifted her seat to face his.

His green eyes, so much like her own, were unreadable. Finally he scrubbed a hand over his face. "God thinks it's funny to have given me a daughter like you."

For a moment, pain pierced her soul until he looked up, a smile on his normally hard face. Before she could speak, he continued. "Are you trying to kill me by going out with Kiernan Doyle? Or worse, start a war?" There was a dark, serious note in her father's voice she usually only heard when he was dealing with the rest of the pack.

"We have more important problems than me dating a vampire, Dad. Someone—wolf shifters—tried to kidnap me earlier tonight. I was really drained after a few surgeries today and wouldn't have been able to fight off my attackers. If it hadn't been for a *vampire*, I wouldn't be here." She left out the part about drinking his blood. Definitely not something he needed to know.

Her father's eyes narrowed. "Did you ever contemplate that maybe Kiernan was involved and only used the situation to get in your good graces?"

She had thought of that for a split second before completely dismissing it. "He set two of the shifters on fire and blew up their van. Besides, I don't think he'd ever work with shifters for *anything*." If he wanted to do something, he was the kind of man who'd do it himself, not depend on others. "And what purpose would he have for fake-saving me?" He couldn't have known she'd be leaving the restaurant early, and he'd been stopping by her veterinary clinic every Friday for the past few months. On many of those occasions she'd been alone. He could easily have hurt her if he'd wanted to. She'd seen the way he lit up those shifters. The sexy vamp was powerful.

Her father's face hardened. "To get you into bed, to use you against our pack. The options are limitless. And if he thinks I'll allow him to touch you—"

"Dad!" Right now she was talking to her father, not her Alpha. "I so don't want to talk about that, *ever*. Whatever's going on with Kiernan and me is our business."

He thrust out a finger at her, driving his point home. "It's not your business if it involves the pack."

"Our pack attacked him, in his home. He did nothing to us or me in retaliation, though he had every right."

"We didn't know that and you weren't answering your phone. Instead you were too busy healing thugs down at the homeless shelter." His head tilted to the side a fraction, almost daring her to deny it.

She jerked back, surprised by his words.

His jaw clenched once. "Yes, I know about what you do down there."

"H-how?" She'd been so careful to keep it a secret from him.

His green eyes narrowed ever so slightly. "I'm Alpha for a reason."

She bit her bottom lip and frowned. "So if you knew I was moving around of my own free will, you had to know I wasn't in any danger from Kiernan."

"We knew no such thing." But his words didn't ring true.

Her father wasn't a fool, not at almost three hundred years old. He'd wanted to make a statement to Kiernan by invading his condo, but he hadn't been there himself. If he'd truly thought her in danger, he'd have led that raid, not sent her brothers. And if he'd been there it would have sent a clear message to Kiernan. By staying back, it had been obvious he hadn't been declaring war.

Sighing, she decided to leave the topic alone for the moment. They would never see eye-to-eye on the subject of one very tall, very sexy vampire and she didn't want to argue with her father. Not when they had more pressing matters at hand. But first . . . "Why did Miguel kill Kiernan's brother? I've never heard that story. *Why* have I never heard that story?" She'd planned to ask Kiernan about it first, but her curiosity was killing her.

Her father was silent for a long moment, his face contemplative. Finally he spoke. "The war between our two factions was over a long time ago, but they were the ones who started it. It could have been completely avoided if they'd kept Corey—that was Kiernan's brother—accountable for his actions. I'll let your vampire friend tell you what his brother did. If he tries to tell you it was our fault or brush aside his brother's actions, you'll know what kind of man he is. And you know me, Melina. I wouldn't lie to you."

No, he wouldn't. Knowing that was all she'd get out of her father, she switched topics. "Does anyone know I was in that car accident?"

Her father nodded. "Other than your brothers, Flynn also knows but he won't say anything. He and Miguel both scented your blood but didn't want to alert their superiors until they spoke to me first."

She understood why. Flynn might not be part of their pack—as one of the last remaining dragon shifters he wasn't part of *any* pack—but he still deferred to her father in many things even if it superseded police regulations. If they thought she'd been hurt or taken they wouldn't have wasted time dealing with red tape when her pack would be doling out the punishment to her kidnappers. "What about the van and dead shifters?"

"The cops are running the DNA on them but they scented at least two additional shifters not part of our pack. Wolf shifters." A soft, deadly growl emanated from him, filling the room and sending a chill down her spine.

Her father rarely raised his voice and she knew that the quieter he got, the angrier and deadlier he was. In the past shifters had gone up against him thinking to make a reputation by killing an Alpha, but they always failed. While he might seem like a laid back Alpha, her father moved like lightning and struck with the viciousness of a sledgehammer. He hadn't claimed southeast Florida easily, but he'd held onto it for a long damn time. When he was in wolf form . . . she shuddered. It was definitely best to stay out of his way then. "Did they recognize them?"

"No."

"Is this about business or one of Miguel or even Carlos's cases?" Since Carlos was in the vice and narcotics division, it stood to reason this could be about him too. Though coming after her was just plain stupid, and druggies and pimps were all about survival. She found it hard to believe this was related to Carlos.

"Don't know yet but we're going to find out. I've got feelers out all over the city. If anyone knows anything, we'll know it soon enough. Until then you'll have an escort to and from your clinic. No arguments."

Melina wasn't about to argue. She didn't have a death wish. "Okay."

Her father's eyes slightly narrowed. "Why do I feel like you gave in too easily?"

Grinning, she stood and kissed him on the forehead. "I'm not stupid. Someone wanted to take me, probably to hurt you or the pack. I want pack protection." She just didn't want to be a prisoner, something her father had obviously realized since he was letting her work. If he hadn't, it was something she'd have fought tooth and nail.

"I don't want you to see the vampire again." A soft warning.

Her claws nearly unsheathed, her inner wolf hating the order, instantly rebelling at the thought of staying away from Kiernan. She was surprised by the intensity of her reaction. "The vampire has a name, and I'm a grown woman. I can and will make my own decisions about my love life."

Her father rose. "Melina—"

The office door swung open and her mother strode in, all five feet two inches of her. "Nevada." There was a warning note in that single word. When her mother said her father's name like that, he usually listened. Melina bit back a smile and hurried out of the room, only stopping to kiss her mom on the cheek. Her father might be Alpha but he didn't like getting on her mother's bad side. And Amelia Rodriguez had a serious temper. No one liked to provoke her, especially her mate. Even though her mom hated the idea of her dating a vampire she'd never tell Melina she couldn't. Probably because she knew Melina would fight it even more.

Right now she just wanted the chance to get to know Kiernan, to find out if the crazy attraction between them had the possibility to be more. Something deep inside her ached with a hot, burning need every time she was near him and she simply couldn't ignore it. Part of her wondered if it was what shifters considered the mating call. Then she dismissed that idea. He couldn't be her mate; he was a vampire.

Even so, her family's vendetta with Kiernan's coven was ancient history as far as she was concerned. It was time to put the past where it belonged.

* * *

Kiernan glared at the smoldering mess in his living room, but that wasn't what bothered him. It was the fact that he'd let Melina go last night. The most primitive part of him had wanted to throw her over his shoulder and make a run for it.

His logical side had known how stupid that would have been. Her brothers sure as hell hadn't planned to hurt her. They just wanted to protect her. Something he understood completely.

He still hadn't heard from her though and it was making him edgy. He hadn't wanted her to find out this way that her brother had killed his. He'd planned to tell her eventually, he just hadn't wanted to do it too soon. Especially since she'd thought he was using her or some shit. Yeah, he'd love to use her body, please her, pleasure her, but not *use* her as a means for revenge.

A chilly wind whistled through the broken glass door that led to the balcony. The sun was just starting to peek over the horizon, creating a glittering rainbow across the glass-strewn tile.

He should have cleaned up last night but he'd been too annoyed to stick around. And too hungry. Normally he could go weeks without eating but he also didn't let other people feed from him. Miami had feeding places with live, willing donors open 24/7. His coven had well-paid donors living on the premises, humans who usually lived among them for a few years before moving on with enough money to last them a lifetime.

He'd have preferred to feed from Melina, but that

was something he'd have to work her up to. His feedings had always been impersonal, a need for survival. But now... he wanted to taste everything Melina had to offer.

At the sound of the front door opening, he tensed until he scented his brother Ronan. Striding out of the room, he headed down the long hallway to find his oldest brother shutting the door behind him. With dark hair, dark eyes, and a similar build, it was obvious they were brothers. Though Ronan usually wore custom made suits and shoes expensive enough to fund a small country's food supply for a month.

"You look like shit," Ronan said as he pulled him into a tight hug. Not all vampire covens were close, but the Doyle coven was—especially Kiernan's brothers. As the youngest, they thought he needed checking up on even though he was two hundred years old.

"Thanks. What are you doing here?"

A shrug as he stepped back, then peered down the hallway. "What do I smell?"

Before Kiernan could answer his brother was gone, using his supernatural speed to cover the distance to the living room.

"What the fuck happened in here?" Ronan's voice dropped a few octaves, taking on an almost inhuman growl. His fangs had extended and he had murder in his eyes.

Kiernan rubbed a hand over his face, regretting that he hadn't cleaned some of it up the night before. "It's not important."

His dark eyes narrowed. "Not important? Have you told Father about this?"

"No, and you're not going to either."

"What the—"

"Drop it," he snarled. If Ronan called their father he'd launch a war with the Rodriguez pack and that was the last thing Kiernan wanted.

His brother shoved his hands in his pants pockets and rocked back on his heels as he assessed the room again. "I smell a group of shifters, mostly male, but one female. A very sweet scent."

Kiernan was silent, not wanting to give away more than he had to. Not yet. When his phone buzzed in his pocket he nearly jumped, hoping it was Melina, then cursed himself for the reaction. He wasn't some randy teenager with his first crush, even if that's what he felt like. He didn't recognize the number, but it was a Miami area code so he answered immediately.

"Yeah?"

"Is this Kiernan Doyle?" An unfamiliar male voice asked.

Disappointment was a sharp blade through his

chest. It wasn't Melina on the other end and he didn't bother to hide his annoyance. "Who's this?"

"Uberto Mazzoni, second in command to Abel Mazzoni."

Kiernan paused, wondering why a wolf shifter from the Georgia region would be calling him. He glanced at Ronan, who he knew could hear the conversation, and lifted his eyebrows. Ronan shrugged, obviously not knowing anything about it. Instead of responding, Kiernan was silent, waiting.

The other man cleared his throat. "It's come to our attention that you are acquaintances with Melina Rodriguez." There was a questioning note in his voice, as if he wasn't quite sure.

"What about her?" Wondering if the call had anything to do with the night before, Kiernan kept inflection out of his voice.

"My pack would be willing to pay you if you deliver her to us."

Something dark jumped inside Kiernan, but he shoved it back down. "I don't need money and I'm still amusing myself with her." Harsh, untrue words he hated saying, but if he wanted the guy to keep talking, he couldn't show emotion.

"Maybe not, but one can never have too much money.... And we know of your coven's history with her pack. That's why we were surprised you intervened last night. You killed two of our pack members." There was a touch of anger in those words, the first sign of any sort of emotion.

So the Mazzoni pack had gone after her. "I told you, she's an amusement and I'm having fun pissing off her pack with our relationship. You should have contacted me before going after her in my presence." The lie was bitter on his tongue, but this shifter was calling for a reason and Kiernan wanted to know what it was.

"So you are fucking her because of your coven's hatred for her pack." Not a question.

Walking outside and away from his brother, he leaned against the balcony, staring out at the flat ocean. Not everyone knew of the violent history between the Doyle coven and the Rodriguez pack. They'd battled each other long before technology took hold in the world, long before territories by supernatural beings had been carved out, and long before sweet Melina had even been born. That history had been buried not long after the death of his brother, Corey. "You have good sources."

"We do." Uberto gave away nothing else, much to Kiernan's annoyance.

"How much will you pay for her?" Kiernan asked. Then the shifter named an obscene amount, and ice chilled Kiernan's veins, but he kept his voice calm. "She is young, likely the weakest of her pack. Wouldn't you prefer someone of more worth?"

"You either want the job or you don't." Again, he gave away nothing of why they wanted her.

"I'll take it, but I want to know why you want her so badly and I want half the fee up front. I'll be putting myself at great risk."

"The fee is no problem, though we require her immediately. Tonight if possible, tomorrow at the latest. Why we want her is none of your concern." There was no room for argument in his voice.

Kiernan kept his expression bland on the off-chance someone was watching him. "Once you wire me the money, she's yours." Taking money from the bastards who'd tried to hurt her made him smile inside. He was going to take great pleasure in screwing them over.

"Give me the bank details." Cool, curt words.

After Kiernan gave him an account number his family held in an offshore account, he continued. "Try to double-cross me or skimp on the rest of the fee, and you'll find yourselves at war with my coven."

"Understood."

As soon as he disconnected, he returned inside to find his brother staring at him, an odd expression on your face. "That was very . . . mercenary. I expect it from Bryson, but not you."

Kiernan snorted. Saying their middle brother was mercenary was definitely an understatement. "Good to know I sounded convincing."

"Are you really fucking a *shifter*?"

Without realizing he'd moved, Kiernan's fingers wrapped around his brother's neck. Considering Ronan was older and stronger, it said a lot for how much he'd surprised him. Instantly Kiernan let go, but he didn't put any space between them. "It's not like that between us."

"So, Melina Rodriguez? Miguel Rodriguez's little sister?" he asked, biting anger in his words.

"Yep." He wouldn't apologize for who she was or her familial ties.

Ronan's dark eyes narrowed a fraction, a trace of bitterness in them. "So it's like that?"

"Yep." Melina was his. He might not have a grasp on what she meant to him or have a clue what their future held, but she was his.

It was a truth he felt to his bones.

Right now he needed to move quickly before the Mazzoni pack got impatient, but something else was bothering him. "Why are you really here?" Yes, Kiernan was the youngest, but it had been a long time since his brothers had actually checked up on him.

His brother was silent so long he wondered if he'd answer. Finally Ronan's shoulders lifted casually. "I received a call from Tisha. She said she saw you out with Melina Rodriguez but I didn't believe her. Wanted to see with my own eyes."

Tisha. The annoying redheaded vampire who'd tried to stop him at that restaurant with Melina. He hadn't seen her in decades and something told him she'd been the reason for Melina's questions about the death of his brother. She'd had a brief thing with Bryson years ago and had seemed to think Kiernan would be interested in her too. Not fucking likely. Coldhearted bitches weren't his style. "I need your help tonight." Now that he knew exactly who was after Melina he planned to take care of the problem.

Ronan sighed. "You really want to help a wolf?"

"I'm going to help my female." Sometime in the past few months during his weekly visits to her clinic, she'd wormed her way under his skin. Hell, she'd done it a year ago and had never left. Right now, everything inside him demanded he take care of what was his.

CHAPTER SIX

As he parked, Kiernan surveyed the empty lot outside the warehouse Uberto had wanted to meet at. It was close to a rundown marina in a part of town that hadn't seen any new business in years. No police presence and no one to call the cops if things got bloody. The perfect place for a meet.

Some humans were nearby. There were a handful of heartbeats in the vicinity—probably a few homeless people, and definitely members of the Mazzoni pack. He scented wolf, but couldn't tell how many were waiting.

Kiernan shut off the engine and got out. He'd tried contacting Melina's Alpha—who hadn't taken any of his calls. He had tried her at the clinic, but the woman answering the phone had refused to put him through to talk to her. He wasn't sure if it was because of Melina's instructions or her pack's. Either way, he was doing this tonight.

To protect her was a driving need inside him, pushing and shoving him onward. There was a full moon tonight, illuminating the water about thirty yards from where he stood. Overgrown weeds and grass covered the empty lot next to the warehouse.

He sensed someone before he heard the footsteps crunching across the gravel of the dilapidated parking lot. Leaning against the trunk, he crossed his arms over his chest as a tall shifter male approached him.

With a whipcord lean build, dark curly hair, and olive complexion, he looked just like the picture of Uberto Mazzoni that Kiernan had looked up. It had been hard to find one—even with technology, shifters and vamps liked staying out of the limelight—but not impossible.

The shifter's dark eyes narrowed as he stopped about ten feet in front of him. "I smell blood."

Kiernan shrugged. "She didn't come easy."

A muscle twitched in the shifter's jaw. "If she's injured, the deal is off."

Well that was interesting. They didn't want her hurt. "Where's your Alpha? Or does he send you to do all his dirty work?" Kiernan wanted to get his fangs and claws on the Alpha who'd ordered Melina's kidnapping. Considering the amount of money they'd wired him, there was no way Uberto was working alone.

"He's not here, not for something so trivial." The shifter's words were dismissive but considering how much they were willing to pay for Melina, Kiernan knew this wasn't a trivial matter.

She was important for some reason and considering they didn't want her hurt, he had a good idea why they wanted her. Originally he'd assumed it had been to use her as a form of leverage against her father, but now... "Did you know she's a healer?"

Kiernan felt the air almost jump to life around him with the pulsing sensation of others getting closer. His senses told him four shifters surrounded him. In his peripheral vision he saw two on either side so he guessed two more were at the front of the car, directly behind him.

Not a flicker of surprise in Uberto's eyes at his question.

Kiernan had his answer. They knew exactly what she was, how revered her kind was, and had decided to go after her anyway. He tapped on the trunk once. "She's in here."

There was a muffled grunt then a slam against the inside of the trunk, as if someone had kicked it.

Uberto growled low in his throat. "What the hell did you do to her?"

"Knocked her out, but apparently she's awake now." His words were so devoid of emotion, he knew what a heartless bastard he sounded like. "I want the rest of my money."

"You'll get it as soon as I see she's okay."

"Your pack members rammed an SUV into the cab she was in." Not exactly concerned behavior.

"That was a mistake." Uberto stepped forward so Kiernan moved back.

Kiernan had bought a slightly older model four-door sedan in cash from a used car lot earlier in the day for this very purpose. He didn't want anything traced back to him once he filled the trunk with bodies.

Pressing the key fob, he stepped to the side and turned to get a better view of the rest of the Mazzoni pack members. Yep, four in all. The most primal part of him smiled in anticipation. This would be no problem.

As the trunk eased open, Uberto cursed. "What the fu—"

Kiernan's brother Ronan flew out, fangs and claws extended. They'd left Melina's bloody dress in the trunk so the shifters would scent her.

His brother slashed at Uberto's throat, taking him off guard. Knowing Ronan could handle himself, Kiernan turned toward the two closest shifters.

One growled and immediately shifted to his animal form. Clothes and shoes shredded as the beast replaced the human. The other man didn't change form. Instead he withdrew a sharp blade from a sheath at his waist. It gleamed under the moonlight as the shifter launched himself in Kiernan's direction.

Instinctively, he called upon his power of fire. It danced around him in a circle but when he directed it toward the shifter with the blade, it was deflected.

"They've been spelled!" he shouted to his brother, not surprised.

Since they'd discovered his gift of fire in their last attack, they'd obviously had a witch or fae bless them. If he was a betting man, his money would be on a witch.

It wouldn't matter. Nothing would save them from his wrath. Not when they'd gone after Melina. Kiernan ducked as the blade arched toward his head, and, claws out, slashed through the shifter's thigh.

Blood spurted everywhere. The man howled in pain as Kiernan rolled onto his back, avoiding the giant beast flying toward him.

He could hear the other howls of pain and, without looking, knew his brother was tearing them up.

A deep, animalistic growl sounded behind him. Leaping to his feet, he dodged to the side, avoiding another rush from the animal. As he did, he withdrew one of the blades he'd strapped to his back earlier.

Slicing out, he barely nicked the shoulder of the

shifter still in human form. At least he'd made contact. These shifters were younger, a century old at the most, and slower. They might be strong, but he and his brother would be able to bring them down.

Uberto was the only one with any sort of power Kiernan had sensed earlier, and he currently lay on the cement, his neck open, his head almost all the way off. Ronan hadn't completely decapitated him because they didn't want him dead. Not yet.

Kiernan tried to dodge out of the way of another attack, but sharp teeth sliced into his arm as the wolf latched on to him. Agony ripped through him, flaying his senses like scorching liquid silver.

Pushing through the pain, he twisted slightly, using his free arm to bring the blade down across the animal's neck. Sharp and deadly, it sliced through it with lethal accuracy.

Blood poured down his arm, but Kiernan ignored the pain, compartmentalizing so he could do what had to be done. Behind him he heard a growl, the crunch of bones breaking and shifting as the other shifter turned to his animal form.

Turning, blade raised, Kiernan sliced through the air, shoving right into the animal's heart. A howl of pain escaped the shifter, but Kiernan didn't allow himself to feel anything. The shifters were no doubt acting on their Alpha's orders, but they were a threat that had to be eliminated.

Withdrawing the blade, he quickly arched up and sliced the animal's head off. When he looked up he found his brother kneeling by Uberto's fallen body. A pained gurgle erupted from the shifter as his throat slowly knitted itself back together.

Since his head hadn't been completely removed, he'd heal, but Kiernan knew the shifter's days—or more likely hours—were numbered.

Grabbing the silver chains from the trunk, he and his brother started trussing Uberto up before tossing him inside.

Kiernan looked over at the other two shifters. One was in animal form, the other human. Both dead.

Flexing his fingers, Kiernan called on his fire once again. Now that they were dead, the spell no longer applied. Ordering his fire to burn, he lit them all, but left their heads untouched. Bright orange flames licked into the quiet night air as their bodies crumbled to ash under the intense heat. Without having to tell his brother what to do next, they both gathered the heads of the dead and dumped them in the trunk.

Uberto groaned loudly, but they ignored him.

Everything around them had gone preternaturally quiet. He couldn't even hear the other heartbeats from earlier. Likely the homeless or whoever had been in the vicinity had seen or sensed the danger and run.

Very smart.

Covered in blood and dirt, he looked at his brother. "Ready?"

"You sure about this?" Ronan asked quietly.

He nodded. Walking into a den of wolves wasn't an idea he relished, but there was no way around it. Hand-delivering this piece of shit to the Rodriguez pack was the only way he knew how to show them his intentions toward Melina.

If they still didn't accept or trust him, so be it. He wasn't walking away from her.

* * *

"The evidence is all right here, Melina," Carlos said, sympathy in his voice.

She looked at the paperwork her other two brothers had slapped down on her parents' dining room table with relish. She might love her brothers, but right now she couldn't fight the hurt threading through her. They were convinced Kiernan had betrayed her and were practically giddy in their desire to prove it to her. Well, except Carlos. He looked like he felt sorry for her.

Which was just as annoying. "So, he received a call from Uberto Mazzoni and the Mazzonis gave his coven some money?"

"A *lot* of money," Carlos said.

"And word on the street is the Mazzonis have been seen around town, asking about you. No doubt they're behind the attempted kidnapping," Miguel said.

"Then why did he save me the other night?"

Miguel shrugged and opened his mouth, but before he could answer there was a shout of alarm from the front of the house.

"Stay here," Carlos ordered as her three brothers strode from the room.

Biting back a growl of frustration she followed after them, hurrying through the palatial home—but stopped when she reached the hallway that led to the foyer by the front door.

Kiernan's voice washed over her, deep and angry, as he and her father exchanged heated words. After a few minutes of shouting, she realized Kiernan had brought Uberto Mazzoni and the heads of four shifters to her pack as an offering. She knew she should probably be grossed out, but she smiled to herself. He'd done it for her. She'd known her brothers were wrong, and she hadn't cared what they'd believed anyway. All she cared about was that Kiernan hadn't betrayed her.

Staying silent, she continued listening as he spoke with her family.

"Uberto didn't want her hurt," Kiernan said.

"Is that supposed to mean something to me?" her father asked.

"I know about her healing abilities. My guess is the Mazzoni Alpha is sick or injured and needs her."

Melina knew that if that was true, the Mazzoni Alpha would have to be close to death. Otherwise they might have tried asking her to use her healing abilities. But if the Alpha was near dying, she wouldn't be able to help him without draining all her own energy and possibly killing herself in the process. And her father never would have allowed her to chance helping him if it put her in any possible danger.

"Thank you for dropping off this bastard. I'll make sure he tells me everything he knows."

"I want to see Melina." Kiernan's words were quiet, intense, but thanks to her extrasensory abilities, she heard him.

Her father said no and as they continued arguing she hurried back through the house. She knew where her father's soldiers were positioned and though they were very good at what they did, they were meant to keep people out, not in. And no one would expect her to attempt to leave.

Especially not now.

If her family wasn't going to let Kiernan in after what he'd just done, she'd go to him.

Using her small size and knowledge of her pack's home, she sneaked out a side door and made her way along the side of the house until she reached the wall corner. Peeking around, she spotted a four-door sedan near the stone walkway directly leading to the front door, and an SUV farther down the driveway. The trunk of the sedan was open, and one of her brothers was pulling a shifter head out of it.

Okay, it was really gross now that she actually saw it. Bile rose in her throat and she had to take a deep breath to steady herself. Next she spotted her father and brother escorting Kiernan away. They weren't trying to manhandle him, but they weren't being gentle either.

A need to protect him jumped inside her, an angry vicious thing she couldn't control. He'd just helped her pack, risked his life to protect her, and they were treating him like this?

Sticking to the shadows, she sprinted down the driveway and out onto the road. Careful to stay hidden, she hurried down her street, only stopping to hide in the bushes in her neighbor's front yard.

When she saw the lights from the SUV swing out of her parents' driveway, she ran into the street, blocking it. Immediately the vehicle jerked to a halt.

Kiernan was out and pulling her to him before she could tell him she'd heard what he'd done for her. Scooping her up, he hurried back to the SUV and slid into the backseat, keeping her on his lap.

He was covered in blood, and his dark hair was a mess. Reaching up, she gently cupped his cheek. "Are you okay?"

"This isn't my blood," he said in a rough voice, his eyes unreadable.

The vampire from the driver's seat snorted. Dark hair, dark eyes, similar muscular build to Kiernan. She'd tried looking up pictures of the Doyle coven online and it had been damn near impossible to find any, but she had no doubt this was one of his brothers.

The other vampire gave her a cursory look, one filled with mistrust and dislike. Kiernan growled at him. "Drive and don't look at her like that."

Despite the situation, she nuzzled her face against his neck. "Is he your older brother?" she whispered even though the other vampire could hear her.

"Yes." Kiernan's grip around her waist tightened. "Ronan, this is Melina," he said to his brother.

A grunt was all the response she got. Well, that and another dark glare from him in the rearview mirror.

"I think older siblings must have that protective death stare down pat," she murmured, just as quietly as before.

A small, muted rumble came from Kiernan's chest.

Carefully she stroked her fingers down one of his arms. His leather jacket had been shredded by what she guessed were claws, but his skin was unblemished. "This *is* your blood," she said accusingly.

"It doesn't matter," he said soothingly, stroking his hands down her back and arms, touching her everywhere he could.

"It does matter." But he had a stubborn, pure male expression she didn't feel like battling. She just wanted to savor his embrace. Leaning against him, she laid her head on his shoulder. Her family was going to be so pissed once they discovered she was gone but she didn't care. Kiernan had protected her when every instinct he possessed must have told him to do the opposite. "So, the Mazzoni pack wanted to kidnap me and paid you to do it?"

"Yep. And I have a feeling Uberto Mazzoni will be dead within the hour."

She shivered, knowing it was true. "Thank you

for what you did."

He grunted and she figured that was the only response she'd get. His fingers lightly strummed on her spine, up and down in a soothing rhythm. The vehicle hit a pothole, but she barely felt it. She had no idea where they were going, and she didn't care. Being in Kiernan's protective arms was all that mattered.

Finally he spoke, his quiet words cutting through the quiet of the vehicle. "I tried calling you today."

"I know. My brothers took my phone." She hadn't memorized his number, so she'd had no way to contact him. "Where are we going?"

"We can't go back to the condo, but I have a place we can hide out," his brother said after a glance in the rearview mirror. He took a sharp turn into a residential neighborhood she recognized.

Without either of them telling her, she understood he was making sure they didn't have a tail. "I need to call my pack and let them know I'm okay." She hadn't wanted to take the time to leave a note in case anyone found it before she'd escaped.

Kiernan slipped his cell out of his beat up, ripped jacket pocket. "Here."

Hesitantly, she took it. "They might be able to track me with this."

Both Kiernan and his brother chuckled, the

sounds so similar it startled her. Kiernan shook his head. "All our phones are encrypted. The number will show up, but they won't be able to trace you."

The certainty in his tone put her at ease as she dialed her mother's cell. She picked up on the first ring. "Hello?"

"Hey, Mom."

Her mother sighed. "Are you safe?"

"I'm with Kiernan."

"Your father and brothers are very angry." At least her mom didn't sound mad, probably because she understood. Her mother's parents—Melina's long-deceased grandparents—hadn't approved of Nevada in the least. Times had been very different back then, when males actually fought to the death for the right to claim a female. From the stories Melina had heard, her father had fought tooth and nail for her mother. Despite his victory, her grandparents had still disapproved but her mother hadn't cared.

"I figured." She could just imagine the state they were all in at the moment.

Her mother sighed again. "Are you sure he's worth it?"

Kiernan was looking straight ahead but she knew he could hear her mother. She answered without hesitation. "Yes. And for the record, I think his actions tonight speak louder than anything. His is a *good* male."

Underneath her, Kiernan relaxed a fraction. If she hadn't been wrapped up in his arms she wouldn't have noticed it.

"Will I be able to contact you on this phone?" her mom finally asked after a long beat of silence.

When Kiernan nodded, she said yes then quickly wrapped up the conversation. She shoved away her guilt at leaving her pack's house when she knew they only wanted to protect her. While she loved and appreciated them, she couldn't stay away from Kiernan. He needed to know that she was on his side and hadn't been intentionally avoiding him today.

Settling against Kiernan's chest, she traced over his muscles with her fingers. "Am I still in danger?" He might have killed those shifters earlier, but there might be more after her. Not a pleasant thought.

"It's possible, but I'm sure your pack will get all the information they need from Uberto," he murmured against the top of her head.

Considering Kiernan had hand-delivered the treacherous shifter, Melina felt perfectly safe with him. More than that, she wanted to be with him, not locked down with her pack when she had no doubt Kiernan would keep her safe.

A little self-conscious that his brother could hear them, but not caring enough to stop, she reached up for Kiernan again, cupping his cheek so that he looked at her. "Thank you for . . ." She struggled to continue, how to voice what she wanted to say. Somehow she found the words. "You risked a lot by going after those shifters and coming into my father's territory."

His eyes practically smoldered with lust and need as his hand tightened on her hip. The grip was territorial, possessive. "I'd do it again."

She swallowed hard, unable to tear her gaze away from his. "I know I left before, but it was only to protect you. I didn't want my brothers to hurt you. But I'm not leaving you again. No matter what." She desperately wanted to explore what was between them and the thought of being separated from Kiernan agitated her wolf something fierce.

She was aware of his brother looking at them in the rearview mirror, but she didn't care.

Kiernan's hard lips curved up into a half-smile. "The only reason I let you go is because they were your family. If it had been anyone else, they wouldn't have walked out of that condo alive." There was a dark truth to his words that made her shiver.

"What about the feud between our families?"

"Fuck it. I'm not walking away from you for *anyone*." Before she could respond he covered her mouth with his, pushing, teasing, taking. The man lit her body on fire and the only thing stopping her from ripping off his clothes and straddling him right there was his brother's presence. Soon enough though, he was going to be all hers. And she wasn't letting go or walking away this time.

CHAPTER SEVEN

Kiernan wasn't surprised his brother had a place their coven didn't know about. It was just the way Ronan operated. He kept secrets from everyone, including their father. Kiernan didn't mind, especially now that he had Melina all to himself.

Ronan had left them ten minutes ago, telling Kiernan not so subtly that he could have a few hours alone with Melina before he'd be back. Kiernan planned to make use of all that time as soon as he finished showering the blood and grime off.

The jets pummeled against his shoulders, the hot water streaming over his body. Thanks to his age and strength, he'd already healed. Even if he hadn't, he wouldn't have cared. Tonight, he was finally going to sink himself inside Melina again. To taste what he'd been missing, fantasizing about for too long. He hadn't been lying when he'd told her he wasn't walking away from her for anyone. Not his brothers, his father, no one.

She'd awakened a primal urge to possess and protect in him he hadn't known had existed. For someone who lived as long as he had, a year wasn't that long, but it seemed like an eternity not to have made love to her.

When she'd left her pack tonight, coming to him of her own free will despite the issues it would cause with her family, it had stirred those territorial feelings he was just starting to get a grasp on and made them go haywire.

Before Melina he'd never felt such a possessive need about anyone. Sure, he looked after the members of his coven, especially his female cousins. But the desire to watch out for her was a different kind of need. It was a hunger. She was so sweet and giving, and even though he'd been annoyed she'd gone to the homeless shelter to help that kid when she'd been in danger, he'd found himself proud of her.

As he started to twist the shower knob off, he heard the quiet snick of the bathroom door opening. Then he scented her. That sweet honeysuckle scent that was so distinctive, he knew it had to be Melina.

Silently, he waited as he heard a rustle of movement—hopefully Melina getting undressed—then the jingle of the shower curtain being drawn back.

Delicate fingers lightly raked down his back before her hands slid around to his front to rest on his abdomen. His muscles clenched as she pulled him back against her naked body in a tight hug.

The feel of those soft breasts pressing against his

back was almost enough to make his brain short circuit, but her next words stopped him from turning around and taking her up against the wall fast and hard like his body wanted.

"What happened between our families? Why did my brother . . . kill yours?" Her voice was soft.

Kiernan closed his eyes for a moment, letting in memories he'd long since banished. His parents had been enraged at the Rodriguez pack, but what Miguel had done had been justified. And there was no way to sugarcoat it. "My brother Corey went mad. He started killing humans—young couples—after the woman he loved left him for someone else. She'd decided she didn't want to be turned into a vampire after all, that she'd rather be with a human and live a short, mortal life."

To say his brother hadn't handled it well would be an understatement. Unable to understand why the woman he claimed to love would choose another over relative immortality with him had been beyond Corey. He'd gone on a bloody rampage. The members of Kiernan's family were bloodborns—born vampires, not made—which was why their coven was so powerful. But every decade they changed a few humans into vampires. Births among vampires were rare, and to keep their species strong they changed those who were willing.

"And my pack got involved?" She laid her cheek against his back, her grip around him tightening.

He laced his fingers through hers, savoring the feel of her body pressed along the length of his. It comforted him that she wasn't pulling away in horror. "Yeah." Back before the leaps in technology and before civilization had spread, shifters, vamps, and fae had all guarded their territories with a vengeance. That meant anyone living in those areas fell under their protection. "My brother made the mistake of killing a shifter-human couple. Once word of his madness reached your pack, your father dispatched Miguel and some others to hunt him down. Miguel was the one who actually killed him though."

Her grip on him tightened and he tensed. "Were you there when it happened?"

"No." He'd been in Europe at the time. Even though he'd been angry at his brother's death, now he was glad he hadn't been nearby directly in the aftermath. If he had been, things between him and Melina might be very different. If he'd hurt or killed one of her brothers.... He fought off a shudder, thankful that had never happened.

She rubbed her cheek against the back of his shoulder. "What do you think of my pack's actions?"

"They were justified." Saying the words aloud was

hard, yet they set something free inside him. His parents had been so angry, sending soldiers out to hunt down any members of the Rodriguez pack. They'd been convinced Corey could have been rehabilitated, that they could have saved him. But Kiernan knew the truth. His brother had crossed a very distinctive line. Killing because of his own pride and ultimately, Kiernan thought his brother had gone a little mad.

Things had been bloody for a couple years until finally they'd come to a shaky truce. Then the Rodriguez pack had moved down south and other than keeping tabs on them for a few decades, his coven had never crossed paths with Melina's pack again. Not intentionally. Decades had turned into a century and Kiernan had never really thought about the Rodriguez pack. Not until a curvy, sensual shifter had taken over all his waking thoughts.

"Did you ever kill anyone in my pack?" she asked so quietly he almost didn't hear her above the water.

"Yes. It was in self-defense, but . . . yes." After a while, both sides had gone after the other with no remorse, killing anyone they could and Kiernan had been forced to defend himself. And he didn't regret it. He automatically tensed, waiting for her rejection.

When he felt her soft lips begin to feather kisses along his spine, his hips jerked in response. His cock, rock hard from the moment he heard that bathroom door open, ached to feel her sweet sheath tighten around him. It had been too damn long and he was tired of waiting. Tired of being alone.

He pressed his palms against the wall in front of him. His fingers clenched but there was no give to the expensive marble.

Slowly, she continued her onslaught of feather light kisses. His body thrummed with pent up energy. Right now he didn't want slow and sensual.

He swiveled, grabbing her hips and pushing her up against the tile wall in a few short movements. She let out a yelp as her back touched the tile, but didn't protest.

Instantly she wrapped her legs around him and arched her back against the cool, slick surface as she molded her body to his. He slid one of his hands up her ribs until he cupped a breast. Her eyes brightened with undisguised lust.

It felt like he'd been waiting forever to see and tease her light brown nipples again. When her lips parted, as if she planned to say something, he crushed his mouth over hers. The need to touch, to taste her, was damn near overwhelming. Her tongue flicked against his as her legs tightened around him, tugging him closer.

His cock rested against her abdomen and even that was too much distance. He needed to be inside her. Reaching between them, he slid a finger, then two inside her, testing her slickness. Damn, she was tight.

Just like he remembered.

He could feel each small ripple of movement as she clenched around him. As he began moving his fingers in and out of her in slow, measured movements, her tongue danced against his frantically. The energy pulsing off her was almost palpable. She was incredibly wet, but he wanted to work her up more. To make her as crazy with need as he was.

She had other plans. Holding on to his shoulders, she lifted up against the wall before sliding down, impaling herself on him.

A shock of pleasure ricocheted to all his nerve endings. As her inner walls tightened and molded around his cock, he drew back. Breathing erratically, he stared at her, drinking in the sight of her. Her eyes were closed, her slightly swollen lips parted, an expression of pure bliss on her face. He wanted to memorize everything about her in this moment.

He pulled out then thrust back into her in a hard, dominating movement. Her eyes widened as she let out a small gasp.

"I've been waiting a year to feel you again," she finally whispered.

Me too. But he couldn't find the words. Her dark

hair was slicked back from her face, not completely wet, just damp from being splashed by the shower jets. Droplets of water covered her neck and chest. They drained down her body, creating erotic little rivers around her nipples.

He wanted to kiss and lick every inch of her but didn't know where to start. Unable to control himself, he dipped his head to one of her breasts. Her nipple pebbled to a rock hard point as he drew it between his teeth.

Moaning, she arched her back, giving him better access. He growled against her breast, earning another pleasured gasp. When he tugged on the sensitive flesh, her inner walls clenched around his cock. He repeated the action on her other breast and got the same reaction. Each time he licked and teased her, she pulsed around him.

He rolled his hips, sinking deeper inside her tight body.

"Don't torture me," she murmured.

He'd planned to drag out their first time since last year together, but they had all night and if he had any say, this sure as hell wouldn't be their last night. "I'm not letting you go again," he growled. She should realize that by now.

"Good." When she dug her fingers into his shoulders, he reached between their bodies and rubbed his finger over her clit. The small nub was swollen, sensitive. As he gently flicked it, her entire body jerked against him.

He knew it wouldn't take her long to come. With each stroke over her clit, she moved, rubbing her breasts against his chest until her inner walls started convulsing around him. They clenched, milking him tighter and tighter until she moaned. The sound was loud and uninhibited, echoing off the tiled walls of the shower.

As her climax rocked through her, she grasped the back of his head and pulled him against her neck. "Taste me," she demanded.

Those two words held so much power over him. For a fraction of a moment he wanted to stop, to ask if she was sure, but his most primal side took over. He was touched she was allowing him this privilege, and turned on she was being so damn demanding about it. She'd given him permission and there was no turning back now.

For either of them.

He released his fangs, raking them over the soft column of her neck as he continued moving inside her. Sinking his teeth into her vein, he lost control and his orgasm tore through him. Years of practice guaranteed the bite wouldn't hurt her, instead increasing her own pleasure. Her heightened moans and inner walls tightening even more around him to let him know it did.

The taste of her sweet blood on his tongue combined with the feel of her tight sheath around him was a powerful combination.

Too powerful.

As he drank, he released himself inside her in long, hot strokes. Her legs and arms tightened around him, drawing him close as his climax crested and fell. It seemed to go on forever until he finally had to force himself to stop blindly thrusting into her. Burying his face against her neck, he gently nuzzled where he'd bitten her, closing the small puncture wounds with his tongue. He'd imagined it would take some convincing for her to allow him to drink from her. That she'd given this to him so freely touched him in ways words couldn't describe.

He wasn't sure how much time passed, how long he kept her pressed up against the tiled wall. He wanted to stay buried inside her, to feel those warm arms around him forever. When the water turned tepid, he blindly reached out and turned the knob off.

Her grip on him didn't lessen as he strode from the bathroom to the connected bedroom. If anything, it grew tighter. That honeysuckle scent of hers was strong, emanating off her in potent waves as he laid her on the bed, covering her luscious body with his once again.

He was so thankful she wasn't in heat and he didn't have to worry about condoms. Since neither of their species could get diseases and she wasn't ovulating, he savored the feel of sliding his cock inside her with no barrier. And this was just the first time of many he planned to take her tonight.

* * *

Melina silently crept down the stairs the next morning. She wasn't sure how long ago Kiernan had left her alone in bed, but she smelled coffee and her stomach was rumbling. Wearing one of his T-shirts that came down to her knees, she felt covered enough if his brother was there. She hadn't heard Ronan come back, though she'd been pretty distracted so she wasn't sure. As a shifter she wasn't that concerned about nudity, but she really didn't want his brother seeing her in the buff. Something told her Kiernan wouldn't like it either. That male was so damn possessive.

When she stepped into the kitchen bright with natural light streaming in, she jerked to a halt. Kiernan leaned against the counter, coffee cup in hand, *shirtless*. It didn't matter that they'd made love many, *many* times the night before or that she'd seen every inch of his sexy physique. Her body flared to life at the sight of him. Her breasts grew heavy, her nipples tightened, and that ache between her legs grew almost unbearable. Heat and need made her clench her thighs together. She stared at the expanse of all that muscle, her eyes trailing down his chest, following the faint trail of hair that led straight to . . .

"Keep looking at me like that and you won't get breakfast." His deep voice sent a thrill rolling through her.

Feeling her face heat up, she met his gaze as she stepped into the room. The tile was cool against her feet, but it did nothing to ease the heat engulfing her. Her lower abdomen tightened with unbearable need. Who wanted breakfast anyway? Before she could blink, he'd crossed the distance between them and lifted her up, forcing her to wrap her legs around his waist.

Since she wasn't wearing anything under the shirt, when she spread her thighs around him her clit rubbed against the front of his jeans. The friction against the rougher material made her moan into his mouth as he dominated her with his.

This morning his kisses were slow, sensual, unlike the fast and frantic ones last night. Eventually, she pulled back, a lazy smile on her lips. "You taste like coffee. I didn't think vampires needed anything other than blood."

"Sweetheart, no one *needs* coffee, I just like the taste. Almost as much as I like the way you taste."

It didn't matter how intimate they'd been, his words made her cheeks heat up. She peered over his shoulder, sighing in happiness at the sight of the full pot on the counter. Looking back up at him, she grinned. "Are we alone?" A quickie before breakfast—even before coffee—sounded perfect.

His eyes seemed to get even darker as he nodded. But the moment his lips touched hers, the side door to the kitchen flung open. Kiernan immediately set her on her feet and tried to block her body with his, but she held on to his waist and peered around him.

Ronan strode in with the redheaded vampire she'd seen at that restaurant with Kiernan. Remembering the way the woman had touched Kiernan's chest made Melina's claws come out.

Letting out a sharp hiss, Kiernan encircled her wrists and gently lifted them off his hips. Maybe she should be embarrassed by her reaction but she didn't care. She was making a claim on Kiernan as much as he'd made it clear he was making one on her.

"Sorry." At least she hadn't broken his skin. Not that it would have really mattered. She'd seen how fast he could heal, and it was impressive.

"What the hell is she doing here?" Kiernan asked his brother, completely ignoring the other woman as Melina moved out from behind him to get a better view.

His brother's expression darkened, and Melina realized he had a tight grip on the woman's upper arm. "Tell them what you told me," he ordered the female.

The redhead gritted her teeth for a moment and her eyes looked bizarre. Really dilated, almost as if she was on drugs. "I called... Uberto Mazzoni... told him the female shifter was leaving the restaurant alone." Her weird eyes flicked to Melina. "It's how he knew where you were."

"Why is she talking like that?" Melina asked, frowning at the woman as she digested her admission. Her words were stilted, as if she didn't want to be talking but couldn't stop herself.

"Ronan can compel other vampires to speak the truth. It's one of his gifts," Kiernan said.

Wow. Melina was silent as Ronan dragged the woman forward another few feet. Immediately Kieran stepped half in front of Melina, blocking her. She didn't bother biting back a smile at his over-protectiveness. "So the other night she called the Mazzonis to tell them I'd be leaving?" It had alarmed her how they'd known so quickly, but she'd assumed they'd just been following her.

Ronan nodded at her, then focused on his brother. "I thought it was weird that she called me out of the blue, so I did some checking up on her phone records and found she's been in frequent contact with Uberto Mazzoni very recently. She's been watching your woman for a couple weeks, but hasn't been able to get close because of you or her pack. It's why Tisha was at the restaurant in the first place. She followed you there and wanted to stir up trouble between you two, hoping to get Melina alone." Ronan's voice had a biting edge to it that made Melina shiver.

Melina hated that someone had been watching her and she hadn't even been aware of it. But she was also thankful that Kiernan had been in her life these past few months, his presence alone a protection.

"Tell them what else you told me," Ronan ordered the female, his voice a deep, almost inhuman growl.

"Uberto's Alpha, Abel, was poisoned with silver. . . . Got into his blood stream and he's dying." Her shoulders slumped and it was as if she'd decided to stop fighting the compulsion. She sighed and her words came out much smoother. "They wanted you to heal him but knew it would likely kill you to expend so much energy to save him. They'd also planned to take one of your cousins to ensure you'd help. Or if that hadn't worked, they were going to threaten some innocents."

"Tell them why you did it," Ronan growled again, his fingers tightening around her arm.

She gritted her teeth as she said, "Money."

Before Melina could blink, a syringe appeared in Ronan's hand and he'd shoved it into the woman's neck. The redhead's eyes widened for a split second before she slumped against him.

Melina stepped forward. "Oh, my—"

"She's not dead, just unconscious," Ronan bit out, answering Melina's question before she could voice it.

It was subtle, but she noticed the way Kiernan relaxed then. There was a slight loosening in his shoulders as he stepped back and wrapped his arms around her, pulling her close. "Thank you for doing that," Kiernan said quietly.

His brother nodded. "I'm taking her to New York for Father to deal with."

Melina was equally grateful but still curious. "Thank you, but . . . why did you bring her here? You could have just told your brother."

Kiernan squeezed her shoulders so she looked up at him. "He did it so you'd hear firsthand and relay it to your Alpha. Even though she was involved, we'll be punishing her. She's not a member of any coven so technically she doesn't fall under our jurisdiction.

But she plotted against a healer, *my* healer. She'll be held accountable." Now Kiernan growled, the sound low and deadly.

Melina's eyes widened at that tone, glad it wasn't directed at her, though she was touched by the protective vibe he was putting off. By the time she looked back at Ronan, he was already carrying the woman from the house.

Once they were alone, Kiernan lifted her up and placed her on the counter. Immediately she spread her legs and wrapped around him. He bent to her neck, raking his teeth against her skin. But she pressed a hand against his chest, stilling him.

"We need to call my family, let them know what's going on." She also wanted to make it perfectly clear that this thing with Kiernan wasn't casual, and that her pack was just going to have to deal with it.

Kiernan nipped her earlobe between his teeth. "We can call later. Your father called this morning. He wasn't happy you were with me, but I could hear your mother in the background controlling him." He chuckled, the sound warming her insides. "They remind me of my parents."

Melina smiled and leaned back so she could see his face. "What did he say?"

"Turns out Abel Mazzoni *is* dying—which we just

had confirmed—and your father has already dispatched a few soldiers to eliminate him and everyone else involved. He threatened my life, promised to do all sorts of violent things if I ever hurt you. The important thing is you're no longer facing any threats. Well, not from anyone but me." He playfully pulled her bottom lip between his teeth.

A shiver curled through her, reaching all her nerve endings. Yeah, food and coffee could wait. There might be a lot they didn't know about each other, but she knew that Kiernan would do anything to protect her. That he was a different species than her didn't matter. His actions did. So far he'd protected her, even defied his family to be with her. Whatever the future held, she figured they were off to a damn good start.

EPILOGUE

Three months later

Melina slid her hand into Kiernan's as they walked up the driveway to her parents' house. She'd moved in with him two and a half months ago—something her pack was still trying to deal with—but today would be an even bigger leap in their relationship.

As they reached the front door, it flew open. Her cousin Juliet's eyes were wide as she looked at them. She opened her mouth, but before she could say anything, a crash and then shouting sounded from somewhere in the house.

Melina and Kiernan had received a few wry looks from some of the soldiers they'd passed on the way up the driveway, and she knew why. Kiernan's parents were already here, meeting her pack and hopefully making lasting peace between their families.

From the sounds inside, they were off to a *great* start.

"Your fathers are insane," Juliet whispered, skirting past them.

Melina looked up at Kiernan and raised her eyebrows. "We can leave."

Shaking his head, he clasped her hand tighter and dragged her inside. The house was surprisingly empty until they got to the kitchen. Their parents, her three brothers, and Kiernan's two brothers were all in the kitchen. The two women sat primly next to each other on high-backed stools at the center island. Most of the males leaned against counters, though they were anything but casual in their guarded stances. Ronan stood between their two fathers, his arms crossed over his chest. He glanced their way as they entered, his expression one of frustration.

Melina quickly took in the situation. Bits of glass littered the tiled floor, but other than that there didn't seem to have been any bloodshed between the two leaders. Kiernan released her hand only to wrap his arm around her shoulders and pull her tight against him.

"There is way too much testosterone in this room," she muttered.

Both mothers laughed, the amused sound immediately cutting through the tension in the room.

Carlos, one of her brothers, immediately strode toward them. He shook Kiernan's hand before pulling Melina into a tight hug. Her family was very affectionate, and surprisingly, she'd come to find

Kiernan and his brothers were the same. It wasn't common among vampires, a species known for their coldness, but she was glad they were different.

Whatever their fathers had been arguing about was quickly forgotten—or at least put on hold for the moment—as Morgan, Kiernan's father, pulled her into a loose embrace, kissing her on both cheeks. "It's good to see you again."

And he actually meant it. He hadn't wanted anything to do with her when they'd first met a couple months ago. He'd come down to Miami to confront her, convinced she'd put some sort of spell on his youngest son. "You too," she said.

This was the first time the two families had come together since she and Kiernan had started seeing each other, and when they'd announced their decision to mate a week ago, Kiernan had thought it would be a good idea for all of them to get together. She'd thought it was a terrible idea—and still kind of did—but he'd been adamant they officially put their differences aside.

"See, it's not so bad," he murmured against her hair as he pulled her close.

She snorted. "That remains to be seen."

As more of her pack slowly filtered in and people started mingling, some of her tension abated. In the end, she had a feeling they'd never truly be friends.

All she could hope for was that they learned to be civil and deal with each other.

Surprising her, Kiernan dropped his arm from embracing her and strode toward Miguel. "Good to see you." He held out a hand, pumping it once in a firm handshake.

They'd already spoken before tonight—though her brothers hadn't gone out of their way to see him, which really bugged Melina—and Kiernan had made it clear he didn't hold any ill will because of what Miguel had done.

It pleased her that he was publicly doing this, showing their fathers that they'd buried the past.

Oriana, Kiernan's mother, stood and spoke, directing her statement to the two leaders. "If they can be adults, you two better get it together." The tall woman was ridiculously elegant and more than a little intimidating with flawless pale skin and shiny black hair. Despite being well over three hundred years old, she looked about thirty-five by human standards. And she'd never tried to make Melina feel anything but welcome.

When some of her packmates slowly began to trickle into the kitchen, Melina felt the weight on her chest lift at seeing their families mingling and acting civil. But the fact that they were sort of getting along was just a bonus. As long as she had Kiernan, the man she loved by her side, she could deal with anything.

Thank you for reading Enemy Mine. If you don't want to miss any future releases, please feel free to join my newsletter. I only send out a newsletter for new releases or sales news. Find the signup link on my website: http://www.katiereus.com

COMPLETE BOOKLIST

Red Stone Security Series
No One to Trust
Danger Next Door
Fatal Deception
Miami, Mistletoe & Murder
His to Protect
Breaking Her Rules
Protecting His Witness
Sinful Seduction
Under His Protection
Deadly Fallout
Sworn to Protect
Secret Obsession

The Serafina: Sin City Series
First Surrender
Sensual Surrender
Sweetest Surrender
Dangerous Surrender

Deadly Ops Series
Targeted
Bound to Danger
Chasing Danger (novella)
Shattered Duty
Edge of Danger
A Covert Affair

Non-series Romantic Suspense
Running From the Past
Dangerous Secrets
Killer Secrets
Deadly Obsession
Danger in Paradise

His Secret Past
Retribution
Merry Christmas, Baby

Paranormal Romance
Destined Mate
Protector's Mate
A Jaguar's Kiss
Tempting the Jaguar
Enemy Mine
Heart of the Jaguar

Moon Shifter Series
Alpha Instinct
Lover's Instinct (novella)
Primal Possession
Mating Instinct
His Untamed Desire (novella)
Avenger's Heat
Hunter Reborn
Protective Instinct (novella)

Darkness Series
Darkness Awakened
Taste of Darkness
Beyond the Darkness
Hunted by Darkness
Into the Darkness

ABOUT THE AUTHOR

Katie Reus is the *New York Times* and *USA Today* bestselling author of the Red Stone Security series, the Moon Shifter series and the Deadly Ops series. She fell in love with romance at a young age thanks to books she pilfered from her mom's stash. Years later she loves reading romance almost as much as she loves writing it.

However, she didn't always know she wanted to be a writer. After changing majors many times, she finally graduated summa cum laude with a degree in psychology. Not long after that she discovered a new love. Writing. She now spends her days writing dark paranormal romance and sexy romantic suspense.

For more information on Katie please visit her website: www.katiereus.com. Also find her on twitter @katiereus or visit her on facebook at:
www.facebook.com/katiereusauthor.

Made in the USA
Lexington, KY
30 March 2016